The Heart of the Corsair

ALYSSA ROMEO

Ebook ISBN: 979-8-9927113-5-6
Paperback ISBN: 979-8-9927113-4-9

Cover design © 2025 by Leanne Bowers
www.creativecete.com

For Nana, the greatest storyteller I've ever known.
Love you to the moon and back.

ACKNOWLEDGMENTS

To my family, especially my parents. Your unconditional love and support has made me who I am. Thank you for instilling in me the drive to pursue my dreams, and the resilience to keep going. I don't know what I'd do without you and am forever grateful to you for nurturing both the dreamer and realist I've always seemed to be. I love you.

To my copy editor. Thank you for almost 20 years of friendship. Your willingness to dedicate time and energy to helping me to create the best version of this book is true friendship, and I can't thank you enough.

To my alpha and beta readers. A huge thank you to the generous souls who read this story first. Your feedback and fresh eyes made this book so much better. You caught what I didn't, and I'm grateful for the time you took to do so.

To you, the readers. Your decision to pick up my book means the world to me. Thank you, from the bottom of my heart. Your support, whether through reading, sharing or leaving a review, drives my creative spirit. Thank you for being part of this journey, and for supporting independent authors.

Lastly, to the libraries that opened my mind to the wonderful world of books. Thank you, our world would be a much lesser place without you.

CONTENT WARNING

This book contains content that some readers may find triggering, and may not be suitable for all audiences.

Content includes:
Kidnapping
Rape
Torture
Violence

PRONUNCIATION GUIDE

To aid your reading experience, a pronunciation guide has been included for the names and places pronounced differently from how their spelling would suggest.

Agrego: Agree-go
Eudora: You-door-uh
Mearas: Mere-us
Molai: Mole-eye
Shryke: Sh-rike
Smythe: Smith
Teague: Teeg

CONTENTS

CHAPTER 1
ESCAPE

Thunder rumbles and lightning flashes in the distance while the choppy sea rolls.

Tobias and Lily slip quietly through the hidden passage in the fort's kitchen. It leads out to a narrow staircase cut into the cliffs, then down to the beach below.

Though Tobias was fearful for Lily's safety on the sea, he feared for it more if she stayed. Commander Shryke was cruel, but it was Captain Staunton who worried him more.

He'd quietly observed countless times how Staunton watched Lily, the way his eyes were glued to her every move, and the pleasure so evident on his face while inflicting any punishment on her Shryke demanded. Staunton was evil, plain and simple.

It made him sick to think that at only 26, Lily had already endured three years at the whim of the corrupt Commander and his right hand man. The poor girl had barely begun to live before she'd been kidnapped and brought here, and it was time to get her back home.

Tobias gently closes the door behind them, waiting until he hears the soft click of the metal latch, then maneuvers in front of Lily, leading the way through the short, dark tunnel to the steps along the wall. The hidden exit he'd chosen to sneak her out of is an old passageway built generations ago, reserved as a last resort escape should the fort ever be compromised. Time and weather had worn the steps; pieces of rock were missing, while others had cracked but were not yet dislodged enough to fall.

Tobias's greatest worry right now is either one of them causing a large chunk of rock to come free, taking them down the cliff with it, and creating a commotion that would surely draw the attention of the guards.

He turns to Lily. Uncertainty and fear radiate from her face. "I'm going to get you out of here, I promise," he states softly.

She nods slowly.

Tobias points to the steps, exaggerating their steepness. "Be careful," he whispers.

She nods again and Tobias motions for them to begin their descent.

He takes comfort in knowing that the worst of the storm has already passed, and while the water may still be rough and there's a steady rain falling, all Lily has to do is make it to Captain Thompson's merchant ship, the Dawning, anchored out in the harbor.

Per their agreement, the merchant would deliver Lily safely to her home on Mearas Island, founded by Lily's great grandfather in the name of the then Emperor 100 years ago.

Behind him, Lily trembles from the mix of cool night air, rain and fear. She focuses on each step, trying to be as cautious as possible, white-knuckling the side of the cliff for balance whenever she can grab hold of something.

The slippers on her feet provide no real grip on the wet stone. Suddenly, her right foot comes out from under her and she falls backward, landing hard on the steps. Her eyes grow wide, then clench shut as she exhales sharply, biting down hard on her lower lip to prevent herself from making any discernible sound. The pain in her left hand is instantaneous.

Tobias turns quickly at the sound then kneels in front of her as Lily breathes through the pain radiating from her palm. She'd felt her foot start to give way and had attempted to prevent her fall by taking hold of the rockface. But in doing so, she'd cut her palm on a jagged piece of rock sticking out from the wall.

Tobias takes her hand in his to examine it. "I know it hurts, but we can't stop now. It won't be long before someone realizes you're missing and I want you to be as far away from this hell as possible when that happens, do you understand?"

Lily blinks hard, causing the tears in the corners of her eyes to roll down her cheeks. She takes a steadying breath.

"Yes," she whispers and Tobias smiles softly.

He tears a strip of fabric from the bottom of her already tattered dress to wrap her hand.

"We'll take care of this when we get to the water," he promises, then stands.

Lily follows his lead and they're off again.

When they reach the bottom of the stairs, Tobias pivots left and they make their way along the outer wall toward the tiny cove. The skiff he'd procured from Thompson is hidden just a few yards away. While he's certainly in a hurry to get Lily to safety, Tobias makes a conscious effort not to rush, eyes keenly searching for anything that moves, especially from within the watch towers. He instructs Lily to mimic his every move, using the large rocks and fallen boulders for cover as often as they can.

When they're safely in the darkness of the cove, Tobias ushers Lily ahead of him then takes a final glance back to the fort, looking and listening to see if anyone has raised an alarm. If all goes according to plan, no one will really notice Lily's absence until after dawn, giving Thompson and the Dawning approximately seven hours to get as far out to sea as possible.

He catches up to Lily, who has stopped at the shoreline and is gazing at the skiff. She looks uneasy.

"You said I don't have far to row, right?" she asks, not taking her eyes off the skiff.

"Not far at all. The Dawning is anchored out in the harbor, and with the storm clouds blocking the moon's light, you'll have extra cover. Thompson and members of his crew are waiting to help get you aboard as well. I know this isn't the easiest way but we couldn't risk the guards finding you in any of the empty crates he takes out of here. Their inspections are random and they're far too loyal to Shryke and Staunton to be bought off if they found you in a crate."

"I understand, this is the better plan… I can do it."

Tobias tosses a small sack of food and fresh water he'd stolen for her into the skiff. "It's the best I could do. Thompson will have provisions, so just a little extra to show you're not meant to be a burden."

"How did you get him to agree to this?"

Tobias sighs. "The same way you get people to do a lot of things… money. Or rather, the promise of it. I told him your father is Governor of Mearas Island and that surely he'd offer a reward to the one who safely returns his daughter. As it turns out, I was right. Thompson anchored at Mearas during one of his trading runs a few months back and quietly asked around. Your father has had a sizable reward listed for your return since you were taken."

Lily sighs. It feels strange knowing she's been a five-day sail from home these last three years, but no one had ever checked for her on Agrego. Although, perhaps it wasn't so surprising considering who Commander Shryke is. Would her parents have ever truly thought that he'd kidnap their daughter?

"I still don't understand how it happened, I really have no memory of anything after that day on the beach." Lily laces the fingers of her uninjured hand through Tobias's and holds it tightly before lifting it to her lips and placing a gentle kiss on the top of his knuckles. "Thank you, Tobias. I'll never be able to repay you for the risk you're taking."

Lily knows that despite the uncertainty of whether this

plan will succeed or not, trying was better than continuing to live as a prisoner of Bartholomew Shryke, and under Antony Staunton's creepy, watchful gaze.

"Come, come now," the old man says softly. "We need to hurry." He guides Lily to the water and unwraps the bloody, makeshift bandage. They kneel down together after Tobias tears another bit of fabric from the bottom of her dress, then holds her hand just above the surface of the water. "This is going to sting," he warns.

Lily inhales deeply as Tobias plunges her hand into it. Her immediate reaction is to pull it out, and whimpers escape her closed mouth as the salt water seeps into the open wound, but Tobias holds on tightly.

"I know, I know, but the salt will help clean it," he assures her.

When Lily finally relaxes her arm, Tobias rubs his thumbs gently over her palm, looking to loosen any bits of grit that might be stuck in her skin. She sucks in air through gritted teeth, but no longer struggles to free her hand.

After a few moments, Tobias lifts Lily's hand out of the water. He passes his thumb slowly over her bleeding palm. It feels mostly smooth. One more dunk, then Tobias wraps the cloth around Lily's hand, tying a knot to secure the new bandage.

"This will take time to heal. Thompson should have something on his ship to stop the bleeding, but this will have to do for now. Once he takes care of it properly keep it dry and clean, and you should be able to prevent infection," he instructs as they both stand.

Tobias holds Lily's good hand, helping her down into

the skiff. When she's settled on the wooden seat, an oar in each hand, he unties the rope from the rock it's wrapped around and throws it into the front of the boat. "Go, sweet child. Row as hard as you can until you reach the ship."

Lily hesitates a moment. "Tobias, come with me, get away from this place. You don't belong here."

Tobias shakes his head. "One escapee is more than enough for Thompson to risk. I'm old, I've lived my life, now go live yours." Tobias pushes the skiff into the water and Lily pulls evenly on the oars. "Goodbye my dear," he states with a soft, caring smile.

Lily stops briefly. "I will come back for you, I promise. Once my father learns about the monsters Shryke and Staunton are, he'll raze this place to the ground, and you and I will watch as it burns."

Tobias gives a curt nod and small smile before Lily resumes pulling on the oars. Lily's strong and Tobias knows she'll do whatever is needed to ensure she puts a great distance between herself and this island. He only hopes he hadn't started her escape too late.

Shryke had demanded a later supper this evening, which delayed their plans. He was grateful Thompson agreed to stall the reloading process to slow their expected departure from the harbor without raising suspicion.

As Lily shrinks from view into the darkness of the night, Tobias whispers his good luck wishes, then looks up to the cloud-covered sky. "Please, please let her find safety."

After a few moments, Tobias turns away from the

cove and begins his short journey back to the fort, knowing that now is when the real danger begins.

~

Lily rows as hard as she can. The worst of the storm had moved on, but the bob of the skiff on the rough water is hard to control. Her left hand is throbbing from the gash and still bleeding due to the repetitive motion of it loosening and tightening around the oar. The pain tells Lily to stop rowing, but her desperation to escape the fort, and her imprisonment by Shryke, keep her going.

Shivering, Lily pushes on, carefully watching the island she'd been a prisoner of for three years, and listening for signs that anyone has been alerted to her absence, but there's nothing unusual that she can see or hear.

Lily thinks about Tobias, the sweet old man whose own life he now risked to help her.

Tobias worked in the prison kitchen. On days where Lily still felt like she had some fight in her and would defy Shryke, he'd order Staunton to throw her back in her room or one of the empty cells without supper. Tobias would always make it his mission to bring her any concealable food he could find. The meals Tobias delivered mostly consisted of bread and leftover meat from the feasts for Agrego's guards, anything she could consume and leave no trace of its existence; an act of defiance and solidarity between two prisoners of that wretched island.

Tobias would often whisper through Lily's door, or cell bars at times when Shryke decided she was in need of extra punishment, "I'm so sorry, you do not deserve this," then quietly limp away. He had no idea why Lily was there, but he knew she could have never done anything so gruesome as to be sentenced to this hell on earth, and after time he'd made it a point to learn her story... at least what she remembered up until the day she was taken.

Lily swivels on the wooden seat to see if anything is visible to her yet. As she rows around a bend and out into the harbor she spots the Dawning. There's minimal light emanating from the ship, but as she gets closer, Lily notices five men standing along the top rail, looking out in her direction.

A whistling sound comes from one of them and Lily responds with one of her own to let them know she's close.

~

Lily looks up at the men while the skiff bumps along the side of the ship. She can barely make out their faces, or what they're saying to each other. Suddenly, a rope ladder is thrown over the rail, the bottom rungs land in the skiff.

Lily slings the small sack over her shoulder and begins climbing. She's wobbly from the pliability of the rope, and pain in her left hand makes it difficult to grip each rung tightly. When she's practically at the top of the ladder one of the men offers her his hand then helps her swing over the rail, holding on until both her feet are firmly planted on the ship's deck. She straightens, looking at each man, taking them in the same way they are her. "Captain Thompson?" she prompts, hoping he's one of them.

A man who looks about her father's age steps forward. He has a kind face, one weathered from the sun and time on the open water. "I'm Thompson. Welcome aboard, Miss Mearas."

"Thank you, Captain. Please, call me Lily. I know this is a massive risk for you, and I assure you my father will know so too."

He nods. Lily understands he's not doing this out of the kindness of his heart the way Tobias is, but she's grateful regardless.

Thompson looks at his men. "Store the skiff then let's get underway. It's a week to Mearas Island if the weather holds and I want to put as much distance between us and Agrego as possible. If the shipment schedule is still the same, two more vessels are due into port here tomorrow. With some luck, they won't know you're missing until after those ships depart and won't think twice about us as your escape vessel."

"Aye, Captain," the man to Lily's right replies and two others hoist themselves over the side of the ship and down onto the skiff.

Thompson reaches for Lily's left hand. She winces and pulls away. "What happened?" he asks.

Lily turns her palm over and unwraps the bloody fabric to show him. "I slipped and tried to catch myself. Smashed my hand on a jagged rock instead. Tobias cleaned it as much as he could but said you'd likely be able to do more."

Thompson examines her palm. "Aye, I can sew that up. Come with me, let's get you settled and take care of this."

He leads Lily up a few steps then opens a door behind the helm, motioning for her to enter.

Lily steps inside, then to the left, allowing Thompson to pass. The room is illuminated by two hanging lamps and one on the small wooden desk at the rear. She looks around at all the maps, logbooks and a single cot along the wall to the right of the door.

"Now, let me take a good look at that hand," Thompson says as he pulls a canvas bag from a cabinet behind the desk, then motions for Lily to take a seat on the chair opposite it.

She does, dropping her small sack on the floor as she sits. Thompson unwraps her hand and moves the lamp closer.

"It does look fairly clean. A few stitches should do the trick." He clears his throat. "I'll warn you though, it's going to hurt."

"Compared to what I've been through, I'll be fine," she thinks, then squares her shoulders. "I can handle it, I promise."

Thompson lets out a little chuckle. "I'm sure you can, afterall, you've survived Agrego for three years." He claps his hands together once, pours some whiskey into a goblet, hands it to Lily then unrolls his canvas bag, revealing some medical instruments that have clearly seen better days. "Drink it all," he instructs.

Lily does as he says without question or hesitation while she watches him pour whiskey over one of the tools that looks like a needle.

"Now, hold still." Thompson sits atop the chair on his side of the desk, pulls Lily's hand to him, then holds her wrist tightly with one hand, moving the needle and thread closer.

Lily lets out a mix between a groan and a yelp when the needle pierces her skin, and without thinking, attempts to pull her hand away. Thompson holds her firmly, the needle and thread only pushed through once.

"You must stay still," he reminds her, holding steady.

She clears her throat and takes a deep breath. "Apologies, Captain, it won't happen again." Lily finds her resolve to bear the pain. She's been through worse, afterall.

He looks up at her before continuing. To Thompson's surprise, Lily's hand remains on the table while he works. She lets out a few shuddering breaths and gasps, with the occasional groan and swig of alcohol, but that's all.

"You did well," he compliments when he finally lets go of her hand. "Now, a clean bit of cloth should do it." He pulls some from the cabinet below the rear window and wraps her hand again. "I'll check this in a day or so."

Lily cradles her hand. "Thank you, Captain."

The ship lurches and Lily places both hands on the table to steady herself.

"Finally underway," Thompson announces.

Her eyes widen slightly. She breathes through the slight swimminess in her head then walks to the rear window to take a last look at Agrego. *"Finally,"* she thinks with her first real sigh of real relief.

"I have some duties to attend to with the crew as we set sail. My cabin is yours," Thompson announces.

Lily turns back to him. "Captain, this is your room, I couldn't possibly accept. I'm happy to take a hammock with the crew or…"

Thompson stops short at the door. "Absolutely not," he replies firmly, turning around to look at her, then softens his gaze. "I don't know what you've been through these past few years but you are the daughter of a governor, a lady, you shall not do any such thing."

Lily opens her mouth to speak but doesn't know what to say so she simply nods her acceptance of his offer.

"Get some rest and I'll see you in the morning," he states while twisting the door handle and exiting the room.

After a few beats, Lily returns to the window and watches the fort on Agrego start shrinking from view. The horrors of the last three years flood her mind as the combined effects of the whiskey and exhaustion hit her.

"I can't wait to watch you burn," she mumbles, turning from the window and stumbling to the Captain's cot. Within moments of lowering herself onto it she's asleep, and the usual nightmares about Agrego take hold.

CHAPTER 2
THE SAVAGE SEA

Lily wakes with a start, bolting upright on the cot. Her head swims causing her to sway slightly.

She rubs her temples with her right hand while attempting to wipe the sleep from her eyes with her left, but the throb of the wound stops her. After a few blinks and a rub with her right hand, she fully opens her eyes. Daylight registers as it streams through the windows.

She rises from the bed, albeit unsteadily, and makes her way across the room to them before unlatching one and pushing it open. The smell of the sea and a warm breeze greet her, and she can't help but smile. There's no island in sight, Agrego or otherwise, and she wonders where they are. She lets out a long exhale that feels as if she'd been holding it in forever.

When she turns back to survey the room, her eyes fall on the little sack Tobias had given her. She's famished, so she quickly opens it and pulls out some bread and one of the canteens. She drinks so rapidly she chokes on the water a little and is forced to slow down. Once the coughing subsides she devours one of the rolls while sitting by the open window. *"I'm free."*

After finishing a few more pieces of a second roll and some swigs of water, Lily crosses the room to head up on deck. She catches her reflection in a small mirror hanging on the wall though and stops. Her coloring is a little off. She figures it must be from being on the sea and can definitely tell she doesn't have sea legs yet.

What's more concerning though is the chemise dress she's wearing. Not only is it dirty, but it's torn from last night and frankly, see through enough to make out the outline of her body.

Tobias had stirred her from sleep so quickly while Shryke and Staunton were busy drinking their hearts out, she was in such a rush to leave that she completely forgot to take a spare garment. "Maybe Captain Thompson will have something in his inventory," she mutters, then takes hold of the door handle.

The deck is alive with crew members moving about, adjusting sails and cleaning the deck. No one seems to have noticed her yet so Lily takes another step forward, bringing her closer to the crewman manning the helm.

"Ah, Miss. Lily," she hears from above, and looks up and back to find Captain Thompson standing atop the deck above the helm.

"Captain," she replies, using her right hand to block out the sun in an attempt to see him more clearly. "Forgive me, I didn't mean to sleep this long. I'm not sure of the time, but based on the position of the sun I venture it's early afternoon."

"You're quite right, just after two, actually." He strides to the stairs and descends to her level. "And no apologies, you must have needed the sleep. I'm sure the whiskey helped too," he adds with a wink.

She nods. "Yes. Um, Captain, I was wondering, do you have any dresses or any other clothing on the ship? I'm afraid in my haste to leave I didn't pack one and this chemise is… well…"

He looks her up and down, as do a few members of the crew within earshot. "Unfortunately, there are no dresses on this ship. Rarely are they part of my cargo, but, I'm sure we could find you some britches and a shirt. Long as you don't mind being dressed like a man."

She lets out a brief, breathy chuckle. "I don't, and it might honestly be safer for me too when we dock at Mearas."

"That's a good point. Follow me," he instructs.

Lily follows him back to his quarters, ignoring the looks from a few of the men as they go, but still crossing her arms over her chest to cover up. "Captain," she begins when they enter the room, "does your crew know who I am and what you're doing for me?"

Thompson pulls open a few drawers and starts moving clothing around. "A few do, the men on deck with me last night, my most trusted shipmates. The others don't know how you came aboard. They were told you're just a woman Shryke decided to release and we're being paid extra to take you back to one of the ports."

"I see."

He turns from the drawer, a pair of britches in hand.

16

"Anything in here is going to be big on you, but I'll get some rope for you to fashion a belt. Take a look through this second drawer for a shirt, and you can use that hat hanging by the door."

Lily takes the britches from him. "Thank you, Captain."

"No problem. You change and I'll find you some rope." With that Thompson departs the room.

Lily starts digging through the drawer. He was right, everything is going to drown her, but anything is better than nothing so she picks a shirt, strips off her dirty chemise and lets the shirt fall down over her body. She pulls the britches on quickly and holds them up with one hand as she walks over to grab the hat Thompson pointed out.

There's a knock at the door.

"Come in," she calls.

Thompson opens the door, a piece of rope dangling from his right hand. "Well done," he remarks.

"It'll be even better with the belt," she replies with a laugh.

He hands the rope over to her. "See you up on deck," he states, then departs.

~

Up on deck a day later, Lily makes sure she's standing out of anyone's way but in a spot that allows her to soak in the sun's rays. She still doesn't feel quite right, it's almost like she's coming down with a fever, and hopes the sun and fresh air will turn that around.

Her palm is throbbing even more than yesterday, but she hasn't mentioned it to Thompson since he's been so busy managing his crew. It's late afternoon and the ship's course is taking them around a beautiful, and seemingly uninhabited island.

Suddenly, a whistle from the crow's nest pierces the air and everyone, including Lily, comes to attention.

Thompson pulls out his spyglass and angles up to the crew in the nest who are making hand signals. He's barely had a moment to register their alert before it's already too late. As the ship sails around a bend, they're on course with another vessel coming from the opposite direction.

"It's a corsair ship," Thompson murmurs.

"Privateer or pirate?" Smythe asks.

"Does it really fuckin' matter?" Thompson responds, annoyed by the question. "We're likely fucked either way."

The corsair ship already had the upper hand between the wind and having spotted the Dawning before any of his crew spotted theirs.

Thompson holds the spyglass to his eye again, looking directly at the other ship. "Fuck," he mumbles as the ship's flag is picked up by the wind and billows, "it's the Savage Sea... pirates." His mind starts to race with the possibilities of what a run in with Captain Teague and his crew could mean for him and his own, especially with Lily aboard.

~

The Savage Sea canons are at the ready, forward doors already open. A warning shot sails over the very front of the Dawning.

Thompson collapses the spyglass in on itself and sighs. "Smythe, rouse the rest of the crew, pull down our colors and replace them with the white."

No merchant or pirate knows what to expect with the Savage Sea. Stories suggest the mood of Captain Teague decides the outcome. *With any luck, he'll be in a good one today,* " Thompson hopes.

As the crew assembles, Thompson calls Lily to him.

She approaches nervously. "What's happening? Who are they?" she asks immediately, fear quickly rising within her.

"Pirates," he replies as he assesses her clothing. "Listen to me, this is very important. Keep your head down, and hair tucked into your cap. Round your shoulders forward to lessen the obviousness of your... bosom."

Normally he wouldn't be so direct with a lady but time was of the essence and if he didn't want his plan to go to shit, he couldn't afford to lose her, especially to the Savage Sea. "Stand toward the stern with Smythe, and no matter what happens, don't put up a fight. Do you understand?"

"Yes, Captain," she replies quickly. Lily feels as if she's about to retch all over the deck but she steals her nerves and begins moving to the stern.

Thompson catches her arm and she looks up at him wide-eyed. "If the worst should happen and they opt for violence, follow Smythe's lead."

Lily nods then quickly makes her way to the stern, standing just behind Smythe. He and Thomspon exchange knowing glances as the rest of the crew take their places.

~

The Savage Sea crew swing their grappling hooks over the rail, pulling the two ships closer together.

While some make the jump over to the Dawning, others keep rifles and pistols trained on the crew. When the ships are close enough, a wooden plank is placed over the two railings and a line of crew cross, quickly cocking their rifles and pistols at Thompson and his men.

Lily keeps her head down, eyes locked on the deck as the Savage Sea crew descends on them. Her vision is blurring slightly and she now feels really unsteady. *"Something's wrong,"* she thinks to herself.

As the crew continues spreading themselves out among Thompson's, Lily hears him say, "Captain Teague." There's clear apprehension in his tone and she wants to look up. She's never seen pirates, or a pirate Captain before, but she's afraid to break her concentrated effort to stay standing upright. She knows something's really wrong with her right now, and can no longer imagine it's any sort of sea sickness given that the weather's been calm since her escape.

Jack Teague, the young Captain of the Savage Sea, steps down onto the deck. He's taller than Thompson by at least a head and much more muscular. He's been sailing most of his life as a member of the Savage Sea crew since he was 12. Now 30, he was in his second year of his Captaincy, and the youngest ever elected to Captain a pirate ship.

Jack glances at Thompson briefly before removing his tricorne. "Well, Captain Thompson, what a pleasure on this fine afternoon," he remarks sarcastically.

"Please, Captain, we're only returning from delivering a shipment, there's nothing of value here for you and your crew."

Jack snaps his fingers, silencing Thompson. "Log," he requests calmly while surveying Thompson's crew gathered in front of him. In his experience, " 'Nothing of value' " more often than not meant something of value that a Captain was hoping to hide.

Thompson hands it over immediately as Jack passes his tricorne to his Quartermaster, Mr. Knox, a man 35 years his senior, serving his fortieth year on the crew.

Knox had grown up on these waters. His father had been a pirate, his father before him was one, and his great grandfather as well. Piracy was in his blood, and had he and his wife not lost their boy to the great fever when he was a baby, Knox was sure he would've been a pirate as well.

Despite his years at sea, Knox had never wanted to be a Captain. "Too much responsibility," he used to say. As long as he was part of a good crew, and could spend his time above decks, he was content.

Even at the young age of 30, Captain Jack Teague was one of, if not the finest Captain Knox had ever had the pleasure of serving. He had built his reputation under the tutelage of one of the most revered pirates to sail the seas, and like Knox, Jack had piracy in his blood. The men of the Savage Sea were either the prior crew of the Captain before Jack or had been handpicked by Jack himself, and every one of them readily joined the crew.

They were a fearsome band of brothers. Everywhere they went their reputation preceded them; ships ripe for the taking almost always struck their colors and flew a white flag before the cannons of the Savage Sea were fully loaded, and those that didn't had found a new home beneath the waves. When they'd anchor at a port, none of them were ever charged for a drink or a meal, though Jack always insisted the men leave something behind.

"To ensure the trust of the people," he'd say. Jack was a smart man, he knew the crew would need friends in port towns so as to avoid run-ins with local soldiers and their bureaucratic leaders.

What the men loved and looked forward to the most however, was that no matter where they went, tavern wenches would line up to greet them, each craving the right to say they'd bedded a member of the Savage Sea crew. Men would sometimes spend their entire time ashore in one tavern, never leaving the company of the women until Jack sent Knox to retrieve them. Knox would never bring himself to ask, but he often wondered why the Captain never spent the night in a tavern, no matter how many women flocked around him when he went ashore.

Jack flips through the log lazily. His ship could use some good cargo but so far it seems Thompson is telling the truth, a few barrels of gunpowder are all he sees.

He turns to the most recent page, which gives him pause. "On your way back from Agrego I see. Making profits supplying that son of a bitch, Shryke, eh?" He doesn't take his eyes off the page, but awaits Thompson's response.

Lily's ears perk up at the mention of Shryke and the clear disdain in the Captain's tone.

Thompson can feel his hands shaking and he tries to steady them at his sides. "C-c-Captain, a man's gotta make a living." Thompson opts for a play of innocence, hoping it'll be enough for Jack's crew to only take some of the gunpowder and leave.

A wave of nausea charges through Lily's stomach and she feels herself sway just as a rather hulking member of the Savage Sea crew slowly walks beside her and she bumps into him.

"Watch it," the man growls, shoving her into Smythe.

"Sorry," she replies without thinking, then stiffens at the realization of what she's just done.

The man halts and cocks his head down slightly to get a better look at her side profile. "What did you say?" he demands gruffly.

Lily shakes her head from side to side quickly but doesn't say anything.

"Speak!" the man bellows, and Lily trembles as the putrid smell of his breath assaults her nostrils.

Before she can respond, he hits her hard between her shoulder blades with the butt of his pistol and she stumbles forward, the deck of the ship seeming to rush up to meet her.

Lily lands hard and a deep grunt escapes her as her injured left hand takes the brunt of the fall, intense pain radiating up her arm. She barely has time to register what's happened though when a large hand grips her shoulder and flips her over onto her back. The sun immediately blinds her and she realizes her hat's gone.

The men on deck are silent; Thompson's crew too afraid to do anything, Teague's men too intrigued by the long, fiery red hair that's spilled onto the deck, and the body it belongs to.

"Vane, what is it?" Jack calls. From where he's standing he doesn't have a clear view of the commotion, all he can see is Vane hovering over something. He does register the look of concern on Thompson's face right away though so he smirks. *This is about to get interesting.*

Vane looks up at Jack. "It's a woman," he declares.

"Really?" Jack asks. He's bemused, and offers a sly grin to Thompson. "Hiding the best part of your crew, Captain Thompson?"

Thompson hesitates but isn't given time to truly formulate an answer before Jack instructs Vane to bring Lily to him.

Vane wraps his massive hand tightly around Lily's right arm and lifts her with such force that her feet leave the deck momentarily before finding it again. She feels so much worse than mere moments ago as the darkness around the edges of her vision becomes more pronounced.

Vane practically drags Lily to the spot where Knox, Thompson and Jack stand, and releases her with a hard shove. Her knees smash against the deck and she splays her hands out to steady herself. She keeps her head bowed, not so much out of fear as it's swimming and she's concerned that if she breaks her concentration she'll lose her already limited grip on consciousness.

Jack looks down his nose at Lily. It's clear through the baggy clothes alone that they're not hers, and based on what he's already seen in the log, he's certain she's not supposed to be on this ship. "Stand up," he orders firmly.

When Lily doesn't move, he adds "Now," in a threatening tone.

Lily takes a deep breath, musters all the strength she has, and manages to bring herself to rise. She teeters, but remains standing, then looks up at Jack.

She's immediately taken by his stature and striking features, as a slight shiver rolls down her spine.

In an effort to hold onto consciousness, she focuses her eyes on the specifics of his face, noticing his strong jaw and short, curly black hair, even the way his perspiration glistens against his dark, tawny skin and through the stubble of his tightly trimmed beard.

His eyes are another story completely. She can't tell if it's shadows from the sun or the fact that her own vision is really starting to darken, but the deep bluish onyx color of them draws her in, and the longer she stares into them, the more a sense of calm envelops her. Beyond the fact that he's a pirate, there's something threatening, but somehow comforting, about them.

"And you are?" Jack asks mischievously, stepping forward.

"L-L," Lily uses the back of her palm to wipe the sweat from her brow.

Jack leans closer, causing Lily to bend backward over the railing slightly.

"I'm waiting," he prods. He doesn't outwardly show it, but there's something about the look on her face, and general demeanor, that concerns him. Of course he can't let either crew know that though.

Lily tries to swallow, but her throat is parched. "Lily," she croaks out, eyes glued to Jack.

Jack claps his hands together and backs away. "There now, *little flower*, that wasn't so hard, was it? And when did such a fair maiden join the Dawning's crew?"

Lily blanches at the term "little flower."

"Captain," Thompson interjects.

Jack pulls his pistol from around his waist swiftly and aims at Thomspon's head without breaking eye contact with Lily. "I didn't ask you," he hisses.

Thompson freezes, unsure of how to move forward with the deadly Captain, while Lily struggles to focus.

"Captain, I," she begins, but the world fades to black and she collapses forward into Jack as her legs give out.

He drops his pistol, using both arms to catch her. Jack shakes Lily, seeing if she'll stir, but she's dead weight.

Knox approaches, picking Jack's pistol up from the

deck. He sees the slightly bloody bandage wrapped around Lily's left hand. "Captain." He lifts her hand and unwraps it.

They can tell immediately by sight that the wound is infected.

Jack adjusts his hold on Lily so she doesn't sink down onto the deck any further, then looks to Vane, who's still standing a few steps behind where Lily was. "Take her to my quarters. Knox, you accompany and help Singleton. I have a feeling we're going to need one of Eudora's elixirs."

Vane grunts then steps forward and slips his hands under Lily's armpits, lifting her over his shoulder like a sack of flour. He heads across the plank back to the Savage Sea as Knox passes Jack his pistol then follows.

As Knox departs Jack surveys the crew, looking for Singleton. When he finally spots the crew's doctor he calls out to him. "Singleton, your assistance is needed."

Singleton nods once and sheaths his pistols. "Aye, Captain." He makes his way through the crowd and back over to their ship.

Jack spins back to Thompson, gaze deadly, and begins pacing slowly in front of the now-terrified Captain, his free hand resting loosely on the hilt of his sword.

"Thompson, the log says you're headed for Slaver's Bay, which is curious because the only cargo you have listed on your manifest are a few barrels of gunpowder and empty crates... I wonder, why are you headed there with a lone woman whose fair features tell me she's not a member of your crew?"

Thompson swallows the lump in his throat. He knew

Lily's wound was infected, and had planned to use that to his advantage by taking her to Slaver's Bay so delirious with fever she'd have no idea what was happening. He'd sell her then sail for Mearas Island to tell her father about the red haired woman he'd seen at Slaver's Bay, collect that reward and sail away having sent Governor Mearas on a somewhat wild goose chase, given she'd likely already be dead from fever.

Jack cocks his pistol again and aims at Thompson, who panics at the sound and makes a deadly mistake.

"Captain Teague, a woman like her will fetch a hefty price there, don't you think? Please, I'm more than willing to give her to you so you can have that honor."

Jack glares at him, his nostrils flared. "Wrong answer," he snarls, pulling the trigger before Thompson can respond.

Thompson's body hits the deck with a thud.

Jack's shot is a signal to the rest of his crew who all fire simultaneously at Thompson's.

When the shooting ceases, he turns to face his men. They may be pirates, but contrary to popular belief, they have a code, and selling people is something they don't let slide. "Make sure they're all dead then offload the gunpowder. Leave enough to blow the ship though."

"Aye, Captain," the crew responds in unison.

Jack spits on Thompson's body. "You fucking disgrace." He sheathes the pistol and strides quickly back across the plank to the Savage Sea. He'll get the details out of the woman once she's awake.

~

One Day Earlier

Commander Shryke bellowed in the great hall of his fort. His men were so quiet the silence was almost deafening in contrast to his voice's echo off the stone walls.

Tobias stood in the back of the room with the rest of the kitchen help, determined to keep his satisfied smile to himself. It'd been two days since Lily's escape. They realized something was wrong sooner than he hoped but so far no one had mentioned her being taken off the island.

"What do you mean you can't find her?!" he demanded from Captain Staunton.

Captain Staunton took a breath. As much as he detested Shryke, he couldn't show it. He still needed Shryke to promote him into a true position of wealth and power, and now Lily was throwing a wrench into those plans. He'd punish her severely once he found her.

"I apologize, Commander. The entire grounds within the fort have been searched thoroughly and I have a team of men in the forest right now. More will be joining them this afternoon," he concluded confidently, head bowed low.

Shryke kicked over his footstool as he stood and it clattered to the floor below, the sound of metal on stone reverberating off the walls. "No, the men will join them now," he hissed, leaning closer to Staunton. "Find her.

Our plan depends on it, remember?"

Staunton's shoulders rose slightly, almost like a shudder, in response to Shryke's closeness and tone.

"Or you'll be one of the next to board a trading vessel, and I promise you it won't be to Captain the ship. Do I make myself clear?" Shryke concluded.

"Perfectly Sir." Staunton bowed, then backed away from Shryke. Once out of the hall he quickly turned right and strode to a set of stairs that led down to the prison yard. As he descended the stairs he motioned to a group of ten men gathered below. "You men with me, now!"

Up in the hall, Tobias guessed Lily had perhaps a day before they began to consider the possibility of a sea escape, he only hoped no one would notice sooner than that.

~

Jack gazes down at the unconscious woman in his bed. It's only been a few hours since they'd blown up the Dawning, and her fever hadn't yet broken.

Based on Singleton's evaluation, it would take several hours more for the infection to work its way out of her system.

He had removed the stitches and was having Knox soak her hand in a bowl filled with a potion from the witch, Eudora. The water in the bowl is now a murky brown as the infection is pulled from her body.

The young woman appeared terrified on Thompson's deck and Jack could hardly blame her, his crew was feared for good reason.

Her skin was still a deep shade of red, burnt from a combination of the scorching summer sun and fever. Her long, red hair complemented her eyes, which he could tell were blue as the sea for the brief moments he'd seen them. Her lips showed signs of cracking from heat and a lack of water.

"What do you think?" he wonders aloud as Knox places a new cool cloth on Lily's forehead. She shivers slightly at its touch but her eyes remain closed, her breathing still uneven.

"I think if she went much longer without treatment she'd be on the brink of death within a day or two." Knox sighs. "What was Thompson thinking?"

Jack thinks back to the few short hours ago on the Dawning and tenses. "Nothing anymore," he replies with disdain.

He accepts that he's considered despicable by most of the world, but takes immense honor in abiding by the Pirate's Code, in which the enslavement and trading of people are considered criminal.

"Keep me informed of her progress and when she wakes; we need to know who she is before we anchor anywhere and find ourselves in a world of shit with fucking Shryke."

"Understood, Captain." Knox turns his attention back to Lily, wiping a loose strand of her fiery hair from across her face.

Lily's body twitches slightly and shivers at the same

time. Faint moans come from her slightly parted lips, the kind that tell Jack that despite her unconscious state, she's in pain.

He pauses a moment, watching as Lily's chest rises and falls erratically, then departs to join the crew up on deck, balling his hands into fists as he leaves.

Unbeknownst to Lily, the Savage Sea's current course is taking her back toward Agrego.

CHAPTER 3
BOUND BY VENGEANCE

Shryke paces in front of his fireplace. Lily has been missing for days now and not a single wretched person seems to know where she's vanished to; not his men, not the prisoners, not even the low level staff. From prisoners to kitchen workers, not a soul spoke up.

"She was locked in her room that night, the men swore it. They're covering every inch of this island... where could she have gone?" he mutters to himself.

"Where are you?" Anger continues to rise in him. He'd worked too hard on his plan, had waited so long to get his revenge on her mother, it couldn't be over this soon.

"Aaargh!" He slams his hands onto the long wooden table in front of the fireplace, rattling the candles in their holders. His eyes pass over the map of the island. There were not many places Lily could be hiding.

The clang of approaching armor draws his attention

and he's at the door to his chambers before the first knock. He yanks open the door, surprising Captain Staunton, whose hand is already raised and prepared to knock.

"Well?" he barks.

"We haven't found her, Commander," Staunton admits begrudgingly.

Shryke balks then storms back into his room. "Unbelievable," he stammers.

Staunton follows. "Sir, I believe we need to consider a sea escape."

Before Shryke can reply there's a faint knock on the open door. The old cook, Tobias, carries a food tray in one of his bony hands.

"Pardon the intrusion, Commander Shryke... your dinner."

"Put it on the table over there," he instructs, pointing toward the table at the far corner of the room.

Tobias nods then slowly inches his way into the room, hoping to hear news, or rather, no news about Lily.

Shryke faces his Captain again. "She couldn't possibly. The empty barrels and crates are inspected before they're loaded back onto the ships."

"Sir, if she somehow managed to get to the shore and swam to a ship, I think it's possible."

The two men hover over the map and Tobias watches as Staunton points to something he can't see from where he stands.

"Look at that cove," Staunton says.

"Where is that?"

"Along the cliffs of the outer wall."

"I've never seen this area, what's there?"

Tobias's hands are shaking. He had believed the men would be searching the island for at least another day or two before they would even begin to consider this possibility.

He's so transfixed on listening to the conversation that he accidentally knocks over Shryke's wine goblet. It clatters to the floor, the sound echoing off the walls.

"Careful you old fool," Staunton remarks harshly.

Tobias bows his head. "My apologies." Then proceeds to pick up the goblet.

Staunton returns his attention to the map. "An old passageway from the kitchen leads down the side of the rocks, and ends just above this area here. It's so old and weather-worn though, it's hard to imagine it's passable."

"Show me." Shryke demands, trying to control his rage.

"Sir, it's dark out, I'm afraid we won't be able to see anything."

Before Staunton knows what's happening, Shryke has him by the throat, pinned against the wall.

"Impassable for the cautious with something to lose, Captain, but for Lily... she'd risk her life to get away. Now, take me to the passage." He releases Staunton pushing him toward the door.

Staunton composes himself. "Right away." He strides from the room, Shryke on his heels.

Tobias is flustered. He hurries after them as fast as he can. He appeared like a feeble old man to the guards to avoid suspicion, however, he was anything but. Tobias might not have been as strong as he used to be, but he was still light on his feet.

When he reaches the kitchen, Captain Staunton is still looking for the hidden passage. He'd found the correct wall, but had yet to locate the entrance.

The kitchen staff is backed into the far corner of the room as two soldiers bearing lit torches await their Commander's orders.

"Tobias!"

Tobias startles then looks up. Shryke is staring back at him. "Yes, Sir?"

"Do you know where the entrance is?"

"Found it!" Staunton exclaims before Tobias can answer. His arm had disappeared behind one of the cloth curtains embroidered with Shryke's family crest.

Shryke tears the curtain from the wall with one great tug and peers into the darkness of the tunnel. The kitchen is eerily quiet as everyone awaits his command. Tobias can't breathe.

"Captain Staunton..."

"Sir?"

Shryke angles his head to look his Captain dead in the eyes. "Where does this lead again?"

"The east beach, Sir."

"I think you're right. Round up some of your best men, take the Intrepid, it's our fastest ship... sail east, she'll be trying to make her way back to Mearas no doubt."

Staunton nods. "Yes, Sir." He begins exiting the kitchen. He'll find her, and she'll pay for all this extra chaos she's caused. The things he was now planning for her… Staunton was done being Shryke's Captain, it was time to enact the plan to make him a governor, and it would all begin with making Lily his.

"Captain!" Shryke calls.

Staunton stops and turns to face the Commander.

"I want her brought back alive." The hatred in his eyes is incredible, and his body shakes with rage.

Staunton salutes Shryke before taking his leave.

"Dear God above, please protect her," Tobias prays.

"Tobias," Shryke practically whispers with malice.

Tobias reluctantly meets his gaze and is surprised to see a pistol now pointed dead center of his forehead.

"Is there something you'd like to tell me?"

~

Antony Staunton stands at the starboard railing of the Intrepid with his palms pressed into the wood.

His icy grayish blue eyes survey the horizon as the ship departs Agrego's bay, entering the open waters of the ocean. The wind catches his wavy blonde hair, blowing it back from his face.

The anger over Shryke's treatment of him simmers below the surface of his skin, as does the fact that Lily managed to escape the island. His mind races through all the possibilities of what he'll be able to do when he finds her, and the absolute pleasure he's going to take in administering those punishments.

Staunton had spent three years doing everything

Shryke asked of him when it came to Lily. He was the one entrusted to retrieve her from Mearas and ultimately responsible for doling out the punishments meant to break her when she somehow managed to switch from being terrified at the start of her imprisonment to being stubborn and combative.

He closes his eyes and begins to smirk as the memory of the first time Shryke ordered him to whip her comes to mind. She'd refused an order from Shryke to not provide water to a sick prisoner. Despite his threats of punishment, she'd taken Shryke's own wine goblet to the dying man and slowly let him sip. When one of the guards from the infirmary reported her, Shryke gave the order.

First, Lily was forced to watch as the old man was dragged into the prison yard and shot at point blank range. Then, in his first attempt to ensure nothing like this would happen again and to curb her newfound penchant for disobedience, Staunton was given the go ahead to administer five lashings.

Staunton remembers every detail of that session so vividly; the way Lily resisted as the guards dragged her up to the post, how both her hands began turning a slight shade of red as she attempted to pull them out of the restraints, her shocked gasp when the back of her dress was slit open revealing her bare back to him.

Then, there was the sound of her voice. The fear in her initial pleas for Shryke to change his mind were unmistakable, and shot a jolt of excitement through Staunton. She was in the middle of saying "Please" when Shryke flicked his index finger, indicating to

Staunton it was time to proceed.

Two things happened simultaneously after that. The first was the sharp snapping sound of the whip making contact with her perfect skin. The other was the transition Lily's voice made from begging "Please" into a scream of pain. The pleasure Staunton derived from that sound was instantaneous and he felt it in his core.

Lily had barely finished crying out when he delivered the second lashing.

By the fourth strike her screams were more raspy in nature as her head drooped forward and she flirted with unconsciousness.

When Staunton delivered the fifth and final lashing he could hear the squelch of the whip against her torn and bloody skin as Lily's body jerked upon contact.

Staunton passed the whip off to the guard at his right, then stood there a moment admiring his work. The contrast between her milky white skin and the redness of the blood that now dripped down her back was beautiful. All he wanted to do now was run his fingers through those red ribbons and taste her.

Lieutenant Rhodes approaches and clears his throat, pulling Staunton from his pleasurable memory. "What's our heading, Captain?"

Staunton takes a deep breath. To conceal that his britches are now tented, he remains facing forward at the rail. "We'll do as the Commander instructed. Have the navigator set a course east to Mearas."

"Yes, Captain." Rhodes takes his leave.

Staunton keeps his eyes focused on the horizon. "When I find you Lily Mearas, you'll regret the moment you decided to escape for the rest of your life," he threateningly grumbles into the wind.

CHAPTER 4
THE CAPTAIN'S CHOICE

Jack stares pensively down at Lily, his eyes narrowed in thought. A million questions run through his mind but all he can do is replay their meeting on the Dawning; the lack of focus in her brilliant eyes, the way she fought her body's sway from fever, the bit of defiance on her face.

He has a feeling that had she been in her right mind, their introduction would've been vastly different. There was a fire smouldering below her surface, and he didn't doubt that he would've enjoyed its manifestation.

Her cracked, red skin has really begun to heal thanks to a mixture of herbs and lotions kept aboard the ship, gifts from Eudora.

Jack slides a chair up beside the bed and unravels the newest bandage Knox had wrapped around Lily's injured hand. He examines her palm, satisfied with the work Knox has done to rid it of infection.

Lily's eyes flutter open. Her vision's blurry and the brightness of the room irritates them. As the haze clears, her heart immediately begins to race when she doesn't recognize the ceiling above her. Her head is also pounding, and she can feel fingertips passing over the gash on her hand.

Lily's first and most terrifying thought is that Shryke's men found her and she was on her way back to Agrego.

"Welcome back," a deep voice coming from her left says.

Lily slowly rolls her head in the direction of the voice. The man seated next to the bed, still holding her hand in his, looks familiar.

There's a knock on the door.

"Captain?" someone calls.

"Come in Knox," the man replies, not taking his eyes off Lily as he registers her confused expression.

When the man who knocked enters, everything comes rushing back to her. She's on a pirate ship. *"They're taking me back!"* her mind screams.

Knox greets her with a warm smile. "Well, hello again Miss. Lily."

His voice is calm and kind, as are his facial features, which remind her of one of the street merchants on Mearas who sells fresh fruit. Both have slightly worn out skin from what she can only imagine are years upon years spent out in the harsh sun and wind.

Despite the friendliness of Knox's face, Lily panics as adrenaline courses through her. She yanks her hand out of Jack's, scrambles to the foot of the bed, then off it, her bare feet landing on the floor.

She immediately wonders where her slippers have gone but it's a fleeting thought as the rocking of the ship mixed with days spent in bed catch her off guard. Between that and her raging headache, she stumbles. Luckily, she remains standing and makes her way to the nearest wall, pressing her back against it for support as she attempts to focus through the spinning room.

The two pirates look at one another then at her. Blood rushes to Lily's head and she sways again.

"Whoa," Jack begins. His intention is to move toward the foot of the bed, but Lily takes a step to the side, increasing her distance from him, so he stops.

She's barely conscious and he needs information from her. The last thing Jack wants is her passing out again so he raises both hands in the air, palms facing her, and takes two steps back.

"Look, you've been unconscious for two days and you haven't had anything to eat or drink, so please, calm down and take a seat before you pass out."

Jack holds out his hand to her, the other points to a large wooden table where some bread and stew were placed.

If Lily's mouth wasn't so parched she'd have been salivating. She slowly reaches out her uninjured hand to him as she takes a deep breath, hoping the extra air in her lungs will help with the dizziness.

Jack is still very much an imposing and intimidating figure, and although she's seen and experienced some of the worst of men over the last three years, Lily perceives this gesture as one of kindness.

Jack's demeanor relaxes once her hand is in his, and he guides Lily to the table as Knox pulls a chair out for her. Knox then pours a goblet of water and hands it to Lily.

She begins gulping it down.

"Careful," Jack warns as he takes his seat at the head of the table. "You'll make yourself sick if you drink too quickly."

Lily eyes him a little, then slowly lowers the cup from her lips while picking up a slice of bread.

"Good," Jack continues, then waits for a beat to allow her time to chew and swallow. "Now, who are you to Thompson, and what were you doing on the Dawning? You're no female merchant sailor, that's for sure."

He looks at her expectantly, the intensity of his stare burrowing into her, and Lily's stomach drops. What was the right thing to say?

Lily puts down the bread while she finishes chewing, determined to be strong. She'd endured three years of Shryke and Staunton after all, how much worse could a pirate be?

She takes another sip of water then clears her throat. "Where is Captain Thompson?" she asks calmly, eyes trained on Jack.

He rubs his thumb and forefinger along the stubble on his chin. "Thompson no longer walks this earth," Jack replies flatly, drumming his other hand's fingertips on the table, eagerly waiting to see how she responds.

Lily gasps. "How could you? He was doing what you asked of him."

A corner of Jack's mouth quirks up and he leans back against his chair. "Yes. I'd planned on letting him and his crew live, until you made yourself known."

Lily blanches. "*I* made myself known?" she stammers through her pounding headache, and finds a miniscule amount of her courage. "I was struggling to stand, it was *your* brute of a man who hit me so hard I fell, revealing me. If he hadn't been so forceful you would've been none the wiser," she concludes with a slightly icy stare.

"True," Jack nods with a playful smile, before leaning his elbows on the table and lacing his fingers together. "We would've gone and within the next few days you'd either be in some whorehouse on Slaver's Bay or dead."

Lily wrinkles her brow in disbelief. Surely this pirate's lying. "What are you talking about? We were bound for Mearas Island."

Jack shakes his head slowly. "Afraid not, *little flower.* According to Thompson's log and his own words, he was taking you to Slaver's Bay."

Lily's mouth falls open slightly, her heart starting to race.

"It's true," Knox interjects. He hadn't planned to interrupt, but the utter bewilderment spreading across Lily's face makes him feel for her. Based on his experience treating her wound, he decides honesty is the best course of action, at least from him. It's Jack's job to get to the bottom of situations quickly for the safety and wellbeing of the crew, but Knox often found, especially with women, a gentler tone went a long way. "To be perfectly honest though, that gash on your hand was so infected you would've been dead from the fever in no time. It took almost a day for me and the ship's doctor to rid your system of the infection."

Jack hardens his eyes at Knox for a moment, but his Quartermaster keeps his focus on Lily, so Jack returns his attention to her and can see immediately that she's struggling to process what both of them have just told her. However, he needs her to focus so he can get as much information as possible to decide his next course of action.

"I'll ask you one more time, how did you end up with Thompson? Did he take you from your home?" he demands, patience wearing thin.

Lily sighs, slumping against the back of the chair. She can barely formulate a coherent thought but she knows she's now at the mercy of this pirate crew and needs their help. "No, he was supposed to get me back to my home on Mearas Island after helping me escape from Agrego."

Jack mouths the word. "Agrego?... Wait, Commander Shryke's Agrego?"

Lily closes her eyes and nods slowly. There's no taking anything back now, the pirate knows who Shryke is, but the question remains, are he and his crew friend or foe?

Elbows still on the table, a partially amused, partially intrigued look spreads across Jack's face as he looks Lily up and down. "*You* escaped the prison fort of Agrego? How?"

Lily frowns as her head droops forward and she uses her right hand to rub her temples. The build up of dehydration, lack of food and this new information have completely overwhelmed her.

"Captain," Knox begins, his heart going out to Lily. His gut told him she'd been through something terrible before the Dawning. He just could not imagine the young woman sitting in front of him committing any crime that would've earned her a prison sentence on Agrego. The place was known to house the criminals society didn't want to be bothered by and Shryke gladly obliged to house them, often adding them to his inventory of slaves. He doesn't recall ever hearing of any woman being sentenced to serve time there.

Jack holds up his hand to stop Knox, but continues looking at Lily. "Never mind that for now. This conversation is far from over, but you're still recovering from the infection and fever caused by your stitches."

He stands abruptly, startling Lily, then steps to her side and leans down.

His scent fills her nostrils, the smell of the sea and sandalwood. After years of smelling dirt, decay, Shryke's stale breath and the sharpness of her own blood, Lily lets the pleasant aroma envelop her.

Jack's tone is low and firm next to her ear. "I'll let you rest some more, but I expect you to be forthcoming with me when I return. Do so and you have nothing to fear from me and my crew. However, if I get the sense you're being anything but honest, I promise you our code will no longer apply and you'll find yourself sequestered in the hull until I decide what to do with you."

Lily slowly turns her head to face Jack, locking eyes with the man she knows now has the power to decide her fate. "Code?"

Jack grins ever so slightly, straightens and strides to the door. "Yes, little flower. It's what saved your life and ended Thompson's. We may be many unsavory things to the world, but we live and die by our code."

He pivots to Knox. "Retrieve one of the old dresses from the trunk in the storeroom for our guest while I have a word with the crew."

He strides to the door, pausing with his hand gripping the door handle. "There's a small wash bowl on the dresser with fresh water already in it. It's not much but at least you can clean up some."

Lily stands as Jack and Knox take their leave. "My name's Lily," she calls after them. Her eyes linger on the closed door. *"He'll either bring me back or help me,"* she thinks.

She takes another sip of water, breaks apart more bread, then makes her way to the dresser Jack pointed out. She looks down to find her shoes resting on the floor right beside it.

The feel of the cool water on her face has never felt more refreshing. Lily stares at herself in the small, cracked mirror that hangs above it and is almost aghast at the person staring back at her; she looks like she's on the brink of death.

The impact of the last few days settles heavily over her. She doesn't want to believe what Jack had to say about Thompson, or rather, that Thompson's intentions for her were so abhorrent. She gently runs her fingers over the gash on her hand. Was there no one she could trust?

On deck, Jack paces slowly in front of his crew. Lily's presence on his ship poses a potential problem for them, one he'd like to avoid. Despite his absolute hatred of Commander Shryke, to make an enemy of him over one prisoner was not wise. Shryke had a large fleet as well as strong influence in this part of the world, having supplied the majority of bureaucrats with their slaves in exchange for power, autonomy and whatever else he saw fit. Everyone knew it but no one did anything. To most there was no point in even trying.

Does he risk carrying Lily to the next port, then let the law there decide what to do? Or, does he take her to Agrego himself, risking his ship and crew to return her? They're already sailing in that direction after all.

Knox takes his place by Jack and the crew fall silent. Jack stops mid-step, then faces them.

"It seems the woman we took from the Dawning is an escaped prisoner of Agrego."

There's a murmur among the men.

"Our choices are to either return her there ourselves, or, take her to the next closest port and let Shryke's influence there decide her fate. Both options carry a risk for this crew. We all know we've been given a wide berth as pirates, and our own influence in ports isn't small, but we also know the governors want us off the seas, and in this region Shryke is just the man for them to turn to."

"Captain," Knox begins.

"Why not use that to our advantage?" The question comes from Turner, a pirate whose strength rivals Vane's and whose cunning and blood lust earned him the honor of the ship's Weapons Master.

Jack arches an eyebrow. "How so, Turner?"

"Strike a deal with Shryke. The woman in exchange for his influence over the governors to back the fuck off for a while."

A number of the crew nod and murmur in agreement.

49

Jack considers the notion. "That's not a bad option," he says aloud.

The crew echoes their approval.

"Captain!" Knox calls out over them. The men fall silent as Jack faces his Quartermaster. "Forgive me, Captain, but I think there's more to her story."

"Really? What makes you say that?"

"She's so young. You've all seen her. What could a woman like her have possibly done to earn a prison sentence on Agrego? That island is a hub for slave trading, with a fort full of prisoners the world doesn't care about... to have such a young woman sent there, well, it just doesn't make sense."

"Her crimes are not our fuckin' concern, Knox," Vane counters matter-of-factly.

Knox takes a step toward Jack, lowering his voice for a private exchange. "Captain, did you notice the look on her face when you mentioned Shryke? She was absolutely terrified. I'm telling you, there's more to her story and you need to know it before any true decision is made."

Jack crosses his arms in front of his chest, considering Knox's view, then looks down at the deck. Knox has a valid point too, the way she tensed and retreated into herself is why he'd decided to end the conversation at the time. *"What could she have done?"* he wonders.

Despite her state, he needs answers, and he needs them now. "Carry on with your work," Jack orders, then departs for his quarters once more.

He's poised to knock when the door opens from the inside. A startled Lily stands in the doorway and Jack's mouth parts slightly at the sight of her in the green dress Knox selected.

"May I?" he asks, gesturing to enter the room, finding it funny that he's asking permission to enter his own quarters.

Lily steps aside to let him pass then shuts the door softly behind him.

Jack stands in the center of the room still slightly awestruck at her beauty despite the rough few days she's had. With the grime off her face and the cooling ointment's impact, her skin has really faded from red to a subtle tan, which he assumes is her more natural tone.

Lily smiles tentatively at him. "Thank you for the dress, Captain."

Jack responds with a curt nod and slight smirk.

There's a drawn out silence between them and it's at that moment Jack notices how loose the dress is on her. "Do you need help lacing the back?" he asks.

Lily hesitates. She'd started lacing it herself but couldn't reach all the loops. She knows the scars on her back may be exposed to him if she lets him, but just has to hope that doesn't happen. As she takes a step toward him, Jack remembers what he'd actually come in here to find out.

"I need to ask you something," he begins.

They lock eyes, neither blinking. Lily knows what's coming though.

"What crime did you commit that earned you a sentence on Agrego?"

Lily freezes in front of him, her voice seemingly gone.

Just then, Knox enters the room without knocking and

Lily jumps in surprise, angling herself so that neither man can see her now- exposed upper back.

"Knox!" Jack grimaces.

"Apologies Captain, but there's a military ship on the horizon."

The blood drains from Lily's face as their earlier exchange about how she hadn't eaten or drank in a few days comes back to her. Surely Shryke knows she's missing by now.

It's been at least a week since she escaped, had he deployed ships in search of her?

She lifts the bottom of the dress so as not to trip over it, then moves quickly to the large windows at the rear of the room. She presses her face to the glass and her mouth falls open, even at this distance she recognizes the sails of the Intrepid immediately. They're flying a white flag in addition to their banners, a sign that they do not intend to engage in combat with the Savage Sea, but need assistance.

Her heart drops to the pit of her stomach as fear grips her and panic begins overtaking her mind. *"This can't be happening!"*

As she backs away from the window, a force from behind pushes her forward into the glass and a pair of rough hands separates the partially parted fabric of the back of the dress even more.

She's pinned against the windows now.

Jack is aghast, he can't believe what he's seeing. Scars from what are clearly multiple whippings cover Lily's upper back. He's seen these marks on many men but never on a woman. And if so, never this many. Some are still in the different stages of healing, while others have already scarred over.

"Oh, my dear," Knox murmurs softly.

"Let go of me!" she demands as she struggles to get away from Jack, spinning around to face both men when he releases her.

She's a mix of emotions and can feel the anger welling up in her, but it's fear that outwardly manifests itself. After a few rapid breaths, Lily sinks to the floor, tears starting to fall freely as an overwhelming sense of dread envelopes her. *"I can't go back,"* she thinks. She looks pleadingly up at Jack, whose eyes reflect something she can't quite place. Anger and concern, perhaps?

"Please, help me Captain. I'll tell you everything, and get you any reward you want from my father, Governor Mearas, but please, please don't let them take me back. I'm not a criminal, I honestly don't know how I ended up on Agrego, I swear. I'm telling you the absolute truth when I say I was walking on a beach on Mearas one day then woke up in a cell on Agrego," she sobs.

Jack's silent for a minute as his eyes continue roaming over the scars still visible to him because of Lily's current slumped over position on the floor. He knew in his heart that the woman in front of him wasn't a criminal, but he never would've guessed she was the daughter of a governor either. Anger at her treatment bubbles below the surface and he struggles to contain it.

He finally breaks the silence without taking his eyes off Lily. "Knox, you may signal the ship to approach. Have cannons ready to be safe, but do not open the doors. And inform the crew they're to speak to no one, do you understand?"

"Aye, Captain." Knox hastily exits the room.

Jack holds a hand out to Lily to assist her in standing. He takes her head in his hands immediately to ensure she understands the seriousness of their situation. The pained and terrified look in her eyes pierces his heart.

He speaks softly. "If I don't let them approach it'll cause an issue, and I think we can both agree that's the last thing we need right now. Hide yourself, and do not emerge until I come for you, do you understand?"

Lily nods, wiping the tears from her eyes.

Jack releases her face and steps back to leave, but quickly realizes that she's holding his hand tightly.

"Thank you," she whispers.

"Don't thank me yet, little flower... Lily. I still have to ensure this encounter goes smoothly and they depart without incident."

Lily releases Jack's hand and he leaves the room, shutting the door hard behind him. She takes another look out the window, watching as the Intrepid sails closer. It's still many miles away, but she begins searching the room for somewhere to conceal herself. She maneuvers behind some trunks shoved under the bed, tucks her legs as high up as they'll bend, then waits, breathing steadily through the panic she feels.

~

Jack doesn't bother with introductions and doesn't

waste any time after a Captain from the Intrepid climbs aboard. The two ships are nicely spaced apart, with members of the Intrepid's crew using a longboat to row over to the Savage Sea.

"Captain, I permitted you to board because you presented no threat to me with your white flag. What is it I can do for you?"

The man pulls at his uniform and straightens his cap. "Captain Antony Staunton," he volunteers, holding out his hand to the pirate Captain. Under normal circumstances he would never extend his hand to a pirate, but he's desperate to find Lily and can't afford to make enemies on the seas right now, no matter how satisfactory it'd be to sink this damned ship in Shryke's name. Not to mention the good it would do to his reputation as he makes his play for real power.

Jack angles his eyes down to better see Staunton's hand, but does not reciprocate. "Captain Teague," he states.

"Captain Teague, I represent..."

"Commander Bartholomew Shryke. And this," Jack gestures to the ship bobbing up and down some yards away, "is the Intrepid. Those of us who sail the seas know it, and your Commander, well. Again, how may I assist you, Captain Staunton?"

Staunton doesn't flinch. Teague had heard of Shryke, but he was familiar with the Savage Sea too.

"A prisoner escaped from Agrego five or six days ago. We have reason to believe she was taken east on a merchant ship." Staunton pauses a moment to survey the crew for any sign of recognition, but all wear blank expressions. "She's pale with long, curly red hair and blue eyes. Have you encountered any merchant vessels in the past few days with a woman aboard fitting this description?"

Jack waits a beat, then laughs. "Captain Staunton, we've been at sea for months. I can assure you that if we had come across a woman such as you've described, and decided to bring her aboard, you and I wouldn't be having this conversation."

"And why is that?" Staunton counters.

Jack crosses his arms in front of his chest. Time to lean into the reputation he holds. "Because, I'd be tangled up in my bed with her right now."

There's a resounding chuckle among the crew.

Staunton strokes the stubble growing on his chin as the thought of Lily sharing a bed with this pirate stirs disgust and anger in his veins.

He outwardly hides the anger he's now feeling though and decides to push back a little. "I see. If it's all the same to you, Captain, I'd appreciate permission to search your ship, you know, just to be certain she didn't manage to sneak aboard in the chaos and confusion I'm sure ensues while you're engaging with and pillaging goods from a merchant ship."

The laughter dies immediately as the crew tenses and Jack stops smiling. He takes a step closer to Staunton, uncrossing his arms and allowing them to rest closer to the pistol and sword sheathed around his waist.

"Captain Staunton, I know you know who I am, the last thing I need is an unpleasant situation with Commander Shryke. So, if I had found an escaped prisoner, man or woman, I'd present her to you. As it so happens, we haven't come across any ships recently, so permission denied... Now, if you'd be so kind as to disembark my ship, we have a heading to set."

Staunton sucks in a breath from between his teeth. He's not quite sure how to interpret the pirate's refusal, but as far as he's concerned there is no honor among them, so perhaps a tempting offer might provide more insight. "All right, Captain Teague. If you happen upon this woman in your travels, capture her and sail for Agrego. I promise, Commander Shryke will make it worth your while. The return of the prisoner is of the utmost importance to him."

Seizing this opportunity to possibly learn more about Lily, Jack pries. "Wow, this woman must be quite the criminal if Shryke wants her back so badly."

Staunton takes a beat before responding. "Yes, she's quite vicious," he replies dryly.

Jack immediately knows Staunton's lying but doesn't question further. "Duly noted, Captain."

There's no hesitation in Jack's response. If Lily was aboard, surely the promise of someone with Shryke's influence would've tempted the pirate to hand her over.

As Staunton takes his leave, Jack eyes his entire crew. Not a single man moves a muscle.

After Staunton's longboat is detached from the ship and on the way back to the Intrepid, Jack turns to Knox. "Have Tate set a course for Molai, and prepare a list of supplies we're in need of replenishing."

"Supplies?"

Jack watches through hooded eyes as Staunton and

his men draw closer to the Intrepid. "It's time to find out what the daughter of a governor did to make an enemy of Shryke. We need Eudora to restore her memories, so we should see what we can trade for while we're there."

Knox hesitates. "Are you certain you want to bring Lily to the witch? She's been generous to us over the years, but bringing someone who's not a member of this crew to her shores? I'm not sure she'll take too kindly to that."

Jack presses his fingers to his temples as he thinks. "Knox, we don't know what we don't know. Eudora may be the only one capable of filling those gaps, so it's a risk we'll have to take. Lily may not be a pirate but she's under our protection now. I have to believe that will mean something to her. Eudora's been fair, she believes in the balance she's been charged with maintaining, so the logical part of my brain says this is the right decision."

"Understood, Captain. I'll make those preparations." Knox departs, making his way to Tate, who stands near the helm, awaiting his orders.

CHAPTER 5
JOURNEY TO MOLAI

The Intrepid continues east, while the Savage Sea turns south. With Tate's plotted course, it'll take about three days to reach Molai, a place so shrouded in mystery that it doesn't appear on any maps.

Ships sail around it all the time, but protective enchantments conceal it from view, protecting Eudora, the witch who calls it home.

Only those who've been given permission by her to anchor there are permitted through the enchantments by spilling their blood into the sea on approach.

As Captain of the Savage Sea, the gift had been bestowed on him by his predecessor when Jack accepted the captaincy. Many years ago, their previous Captain had saved Eudora's life, and had been granted the right of passage through the barrier as thanks. Her only condition was that it pass secretly from Captain to Captain as a measure of protection. Jack had trusted

Knox with the details knowing he would take them to his grave.

Knox understands that the men are curious about their destination, and how Jack had become acquainted with the witch, but it wasn't his tale to tell, so as quartermaster, he made sure in no uncertain terms that no questions were asked, especially from any new crew members. Afterall, loyalty to the ship came with the understanding that you wouldn't know everything.

Vane was the only crew member to voice opposition to Jack's decision to keep Lily a secret from Staunton. He'd begun to protest when Jack first announced his plan, but quickly shut up after Jack's only reply was an icy glare. He'd been completing his work in silence since, stewing over the risks he felt his Captain was taking by not just dropping Lily at the nearest port. The risk to their safety the longer they had her would only increase, especially with that Captain Staunton in pursuit of her.

Lily cautiously emerges on deck for the first time since she was brought aboard.

Jack had given her the okay to come out from under the bed when the ships parted ways, but out of an abundance of caution she'd waited to come on deck until after the Intrepid was miles away.

She takes a deep breath and closes her eyes, inhaling the fresh salt air. The cool wind mixed with the smell of the sea is a wonderful, freeing feeling after three years trapped behind fort walls, only able to stare longingly at the shades of blue and ocean currents that could carry her home.

When Jack had informed her of his decision to go to Molai she'd let emotion get the best of her and hugged him tightly. The hug was the type of human contact that had been missing from her life for years, and she didn't want to let go, but she could sense Jack's discomfort, his body was rigid, and he didn't wrap either arm around her, so she'd released him relatively quickly.

"Miss. Lily," Knox calls from the helm.

She opens her eyes and looks at him. Knox has both hands on the wheel and uses his head to motion for her to join him.

As she's about to cross the deck, Vane steps in her path. They both pause for a moment, eyes locked on one another. He casts an angry glare that makes Lily feel about the size of a child. Without the effects of infection and glare of the sun, Lily's able to really get a good look at him. Vane looks even more intimidating than she remembers from the Dawning. It's like he's a bear personified. His gruff face contains a huge scar that curves from the middle of his right cheek, up around his eye and through his eyebrow. The paler shade of it stands out against his deeply tan skin.

The same goes for his wide, bare chest and extremely thick, muscled arms. He's without his shirt, providing Lily the opportunity to take in his entire upper body, which is a canvas of tattoos and scars blended together in a way she perceives to be both terrifying and beautiful. Physically, his build exudes danger, which she knows is what he wants, but what covers his skin is the story of his life and to Lily, there's a beauty in that.

She clears her throat. "I wanted to thank you. I wasn't

in my right state of mind on the Dawning, so I didn't realize it at the time, but, what you did saved my life... even though I'm sure that wasn't your intention." She smiles tentatively. "I'm extremely grateful."

He continues to glare at her, doesn't utter a word, then goes on his way, disappearing below deck.

Lily looks after him, teetering on the verge of saying more but unsure of what good it will do.

"Don't worry about Vane," Knox assures her when she reaches him. "He's a calculating man, great when it comes to strategy, but sometimes I think he believes his influence with the Captain is stronger than it actually is."

Lily observes as Knox watches the needle of the compass in front of him shift slightly. He spins the wheel starboard until the spoke above his left hand is in his right, and the needle adjusts to point south again. "Easy, huh?" he chuckles.

She smiles. "You certainly make it seem so."

A young deckhand approaches from behind, tapping her on the shoulder. When she faces him, he removes his cap and bows. "I'm George."

Lily blushes at the fact that a pirate just bowed to her, but curtsies all the same. Her mother raised her to be a proper lady afterall.

Despite what she'd been told about pirates, this crew was nothing like she expected them to be... at least partially. Jack's tone of voice and air of command over the crew left no doubt he was in charge. And the crew? They certainly looked the part. Although she could barely remember anything that happened on the Dawning, she knew they'd disposed of Thompson and his entire crew. Lily was keenly aware that she was surrounded by killers, however, she couldn't help but notice that the man standing in front of her seemed out of place.

George was a bit tall and gangly. She figured he was easily still in his teen years based on his young face that didn't show the same wear some of the others had from spending years in the elements on the open water.

"George, take the wheel," Knox interrupts.

"Aye, Quartermaster." George grins boyishly at Lily, then takes Knox's place.

Knox rolls his eyes at George then holds out his arm to Lily. "Walk with me."

She loops her arm through his and the two descend the stairs, slowly making their way across the deck to the bow of the ship.

"I know," he begins, speaking in a hushed tone while men pass around them pulling lines, scrubbing the deck, and knotting rope. "We're not the sort of pirates you were expecting."

She shrugs. "I honestly didn't think I'd ever meet a pirate, and all I've ever heard was little tales here and there, so I truly didn't know what to expect. My father kept any discussion of island business or the seas far from my *delicate* ears," she says sarcastically. "If only he knew what I've heard since," she concludes, almost absentmindedly.

Knox registers her statement but decides it's not his place to ask more about her experience on Agrego. The scars he'd briefly seen were horrible, and he still couldn't believe that she'd endured the whippings he knew had caused them.

"I'll tell you a secret about the crew of the Savage Sea. The reputation we have is one built on generations of seafaring. There was a time when the entire crew of this ship were as mean, heartless and cutthroat as the stories suggest, but here's the thing about reputations, once they're set and people believe every word that's spoken about you, they're too afraid to question anything. Don't misunderstand, the men on this ship act when the situation calls for it - like on the Dawning - and men like Vane and Turner are here because of their strength and fighting, and controlled, ruthless abilities, but most just love the adventure of sailing the seas, living outside of society's bounds, and fighting back in our own way against the unbalanced scales of justice."

Knox pauses as he watches Lily digest that information, then continues. "We do what we must to survive and ensure those who need our help receive it."

They stand at the bow of the ship. Lily stares out at the sunset, considering what Knox has just told her. After a few moments she looks at him. "So, you're vigilantes."

A slight chuckle forms in his throat. "We don't consider ourselves vigilantes, but if that helps you better understand what we do, then that works."

"What about Captain Teague?"

"What about him?

"How did he become Captain? Most merchant and military ship Captains I've ever seen are much older."

Knox nods while he carefully considers how to respond. Jack's story was his alone to tell and Knox knows how much his Captain despises his origin. "The Captain comes from a long line of pirates. He's been part of the brotherhood pretty much his entire life. The crew voted Jack in as Captain after his predecessor decided it was time to retire. He loved Jack, and when Jack proved he had what it took to be a leader, he was all too happy to provide the tutelage Jack would need to win over the crew. He's one of the most respected pirates on the high seas because he does what needs to be done, takes care of his crew, and abides by the code. Pirates don't have a governing hierarchy like you do with an emperor, but if we did, Captain Teague would be a king."

Lily nods thoughtfully. "You really care for him, don't you?"

Knox nods like a proud father. "I do. He's like a son to me and my wife."

"You're married?"

A broad smile forms on his face. "Thirty years to a wonderful woman with strength and patience beyond belief and more than I deserve."

Lily's eyes soften with happiness for him. She knew nothing about pirates and her curiosity about them and their lives was growing.

"This is a hard life, not for the faint of heart, either as a member of a crew or being the family of one. We're gone for months at a time, it takes a special woman to live that life."

The two of them turn to watch the sunset in silence until Knox excuses himself to talk to the night helmsman.

Lily stays at the bow while the sun sinks below the horizon, its light glittering off the water like gold. She thinks about what Knox said regarding the crew, but mostly, she thinks about Jack Teague and the tiny glimpse into his past she'd been offered. There's a strong desire within her to know more.

"So serious."

The playful observation pulls Lily from her thoughts and she turns to see Jack standing a few steps behind her, leaning against the front mast.

"Anything you care to share?" he prods.

She shakes her head as Jack steps up beside her. "I see you appreciate true beauty," he continues, tilting his chin up toward the sunset. "It really is something to behold, I never tire of it."

"Indeed. It's even more beautiful observing it on the water than from the shore."

They stand side-by-side, eyes fixed to the west. Lily desperately wants to ask Jack about himself, but she doesn't want to push her luck. She's a refugee on his ship, and the last thing she needs is to give him a reason to turn her over to anyone but her father.

She glances up at him twice, her curiosity building as she fights the urge to ask him anything. The second time she does, she swears he's looking at her as well, and she isn't wrong.

Jack is incredibly intrigued by Lily. No one had ever instilled in him the desire to know more about them the way she did.

He understands why this desire exists though; an escaped prisoner of Agrego, whose memories seem to be incomplete, and who is now being hunted down by the commander of that island, is aboard his ship. How could he not be intrigued? "How are you feeling?"

Lily lifts her left hand to show him. "Much better, thank you. My hand barely hurts anymore and I feel like myself again. When we get to Mearas, I'll replace any supplies you used to cure me."

Jack gently passes his thumb over the healing cut on her palm. "No need. Besides, what we used can't be obtained at any port market."

"What do you mean? Why not?" Lily removes her hand from below his.

"The concoction Knox and Singleton used to extract the infection from your body was a gift from a witch, Eudora. She's who we're on our way to see."

Jack notices Lily stiffening. "Met a witch before, have you?"

"You could say that. Although, I'd argue it was more of a forced introduction than a willing one." Her eyes get a little misty at the memory. "I don't remember my first days on Agrego, but I remember her, which I'm sure was part of Shryke's plan."

Jack clears his throat, time to push for information. "Speaking of, we need to continue our conversation. You promised details and I must know them before we get to Molai so I know how to present my request to Eudora."

Lily takes a deep breath and nods. "I did." She turns from the bow as Jack leans back against the mast.

"Three years ago I was walking along one of the smaller beaches on Mearas. I'd snuck away from the house, just wanting some time away from the monotony of my life… the piano lessons, needlepoint, boring afternoon teas my mother hosted almost daily, pretending I cared about the mundane topics the ladies discussed, like flower arranging, dinner hosting, the marriage mart." She shakes her head. "They'd talk around me but also about me, do you know what I mean?"

"I do."

"I finally reached a point where I couldn't stand it anymore. These women would talk about their sons like they were gifts to the world, and joked aloud how I'd ever decide which to marry, or if my father would choose for me." Lily chortles. "In their desire to push their peacock sons on me, the thought of marrying any of them made me sick. I'd spent my life around these *boys*, but all they cared about was that I was a governor's daughter. Not one of them ever cared what I thought, or what I wanted my life to be."

"And what did you want your life to be?"

She pauses. "I wasn't entirely sure. But, I knew that if I was going to marry, I wanted to marry a man who valued me for who I am, not what I am; the fact that I was well-read, that I could do more than host dinners, manage a house and bear his children. Someone who could and would challenge me, and I him. I knew what the world expected from women in my position outside of the home, but inside, inside I wanted a man who respected my brain, even if he could only tell me so when we were alone."

Jack scoffs.

Lily snaps her eyes to his. "What? Is that too much to ask for?"

He shakes his head slowly, his gaze steady and focused. "No, it's too little."

Lily looks at him questioningly. This is the first time someone responded in that way. Her parents had always dismissed her expressed desires, especially her mother.

Jack takes a purposeful step toward her. "A real man wouldn't be afraid of people's perceptions. He'd show you off proudly, engage you in conversation no matter who was around, without hesitation. And, he'd know he was the lucky one, because *you* chose him. A real man would declare in front of anyone how much he loves you... all of you."

Lily's surprised by Jack's statement, but the feeling quickly turns to shame at the realization that she'd presumed a pirate wouldn't think that way.

He cocks an eyebrow at her as if he can read her mind. "My words surprise you."

Lily starts to deny it then stops. It'd be an insult to him to lie and negatively impact any trust she may be building with him. "I apologize. Of all the things I've learned, I'm afraid my knowledge of how pirates view the world is practically non-existent, and I can say with certainty that the little I do know is biased, based solely on conversations I've overheard between my father and other government officials."

A slight smile dances across his lips. He's impressed by her willingness to admit this. "Well, I can't say that this is news to me, not everything people know of us is wrong, but it's far from a full picture. We do what we need to in order to survive, and adhere to a code that has been around for generations. But, I digress, we're not here to discuss the history of piracy right now, so back to you. Please."

Lily clears her throat. "Uh, right. So, I was down at the beach. I reached down to pick up a shell along the water's edge, and... that's it."

"That's what?"

"That's the last thing I remember. The next memory I have is being strapped to a table-like contraption in a stone room with no windows."

Lily prepares as best she can for the next bit of the story. "My arms and legs were tied down, and there was what felt like a metal rod over the middle of my forehead, holding my head in place." She sweeps her finger across her forehead to show Jack about where it was. "Out of the corner of my eye I could see a fire was lit in a fireplace and there was a wooden table a few feet in front of it with vials scattered about."

She shakes her head, "I don't know how many exactly, but I clearly remember the stone bowl sitting on the center of the table."

"And you don't know how you got into the room?"

"No idea. I started to struggle against the bonds, and that's when she appeared at my side."

"Who?"

Lily narrows her eyes in concentration. "This older woman with hair dark as a starless night, eyes with no irises or pupils, they were completely clouded over in white. Her face was pallid and ugh, her breath; it was so stale." She pauses, mind and body wracked with apprehension.

Jack notices. He needs this information, but seeing her visceral reaction the longer she speaks, the more his heart goes out to her. "Do you need to stop?"

Lily shakes her head. "No, let's get this over with. When she spoke, her voice was airy and soft, almost disembodied slightly. She commented on my being awake then she looked across the room and shortly after, Shryke stepped into my field of vision. I don't know if there was any sort of conversation between the two of them or with me. My instinct is yes and that she removed what was said as well. The next thing I remember is the look on Shryke's face when she told him it was time. The bastard was almost giddy with excitement."

Lily's body trembles. "I watched her walk over to the table and sprinkle what looked like sand into the bowl. There was a spark of light followed by wisps of smoke that rose out of it before she picked it up off the table and brought it over to me. I clamped my mouth shut immediately but Shryke pinched my nose and eventually I was forced to open my mouth to breathe. When I did, he gripped my lower jaw with his free hand and the witch poured the contents of the bowl into my mouth. It burned so badly and I couldn't breathe."

Lily places her fingers at the midpoint of her throat. "The liquid felt like it was just sitting right here. I was thrashing so hard against the restraints but it didn't matter."

Her voice gets raspy the way it does when someone's trying to hold back tears, and the anger within Jack reaches the point where adrenaline is now coursing through him, causing a slight tremble in his extremities. He crosses his arms over his chest to prevent Lily from noticing. He's focused on her story, but regret over his decision to let Captain Staunton disembark the ship is seeping through every fiber of his being.

"Suddenly, there was this ball of bright light that sort of floated out of my mouth and hovered above my head. When that happened I felt like I could breathe again. The witch whispered something, but I couldn't understand it, I think it was another language. As she did, these black rings of smoke wrapped themselves around the ball of light. When she finished, it descended back into my mouth and the choking sensation started again."

Lily lets her head hang forward for a breath then looks back up at Jack. "The next thing I remember is waking up on the dirty floor of a cell in the fort. My shouts were ignored almost a full day before guards took me from the cell and dropped me at Shryke's feet in the main hall. I pleaded with him to tell me what had happened, what I'd done to be brought there, and why I couldn't remember anything between the beach and the witch, and then the witch and the cell. He never answered me, just kept saying it was my mother's fault."

Lily's eyes mist over. "He had them throw me back in that cell where I stayed for three days before I was given a meal. Then back to Shryke I went, where he detailed how I'd work to appease him for what my mother had done. It's been three years and I still have no idea what he meant."

Jack tenses. "Work to appease him?"

Lily takes a deep breath, wiping the mist from her eyes. "I was a servant. Did a lot of cleaning, served him his meals, was there whenever he felt I deserved to withstand a slew of insults or physical punishment."

"Did he ever force him…"

"No," Lily blurts out before Jack can finish asking his question. She places her left hand on her hip then takes a deep breath while pinching the bridge of her nose. "I was terrified something like that would happen, but he didn't. And, he made it clear to his men that I was never to be touched. I don't know why Shryke drew the line there, but I'm grateful for that at least." She looks up at the sky. "He wasn't shy about the beatings, but that was as far as he'd go in terms of 'ruining' me."

"Is that his handiwork on your back?"

Lily looks back at Jack, but it's almost as if she's looking through him. "No, he preferred to watch that. What you saw is courtesy of Captain Staunton. When I finally started to disobey or fight back, Shryke tasked Staunton with punishing me. And Staunton… Well, let's just say he doesn't need instruction on how to inflict pain; he's a master at it. It took me a while to notice, but eventually I saw there was something in his eyes during those sessions. He truly enjoyed what he was doing, there was a clear sense of satisfaction emanating from him every time."

Lily wraps her arms around her waist like a hug in an act of self-comfort; her gaze remains distant as she continues recounting her life on Agrego. "The only times I didn't see as much of that glint of something sinister was when I finally built up the resolve to stop crying out. It took everything I had, but I refused to scream, and that made both of them so angry, Staunton more so than Shryke I think." She sighs. "I paid for my defiance for a time of course, but the longer I went without crying out, the more I saw that glimmer of disgusting joy disappear from Staunton's eyes, and that made it worth it. He always threatened that he'd make me do it again, but it never happened."

Jack shakes his head slowly, his fingernails digging into his palms as he restrains himself. The rage within at her treatment is boiling over and it's taking everything in him to not have Tate set a course straight for Agrego so he can burn it to the ground, then run both Shryke and Staunton through with his favorite sword before offering their heads to Lily on a silver platter. He and his mother were not strangers to an abusive man, so he held an extra special bit of hate in his heart for them. "I'm so sorry that happened to you," he manages to say calmly.

"Do you really think this witch of yours can help me?" Lily presses, hoping she's told him enough.

"Well, she's not *my* witch, but yes, I do think she can help."

"And do you trust her?"

"With my life."

Lily huffs slightly. "Must be nice."

Jack looks at her quizzically. "The world's witches have immense power and are tasked with maintaining the delicate balance of life. What we know as things like good and evil, life and death, rain and drought, peace and war, they're all tied together, tragic as that may be. They answer to no one and their importance should not be taken lightly."

Lily crosses her arms over her chest, the fire of anger invading her eyes as her face hardens. "Well, someone should remind the witch I encountered what her purpose is, because I'd say that what she did was far from protecting me or keeping any sort of balance."

With that she turns her back on Jack and faces out the front of the bow again, resting one hand on the wood, and the other on her forehead.

Jack slowly moves up next to her again then places his hand over hers. "You're right, I'm sorry. We'll find out what happened, I promise."

Lily sighs. "I believe you." She pauses briefly before deciding to risk getting an answer to the question she wants answered most. "Captain Teague, may I ask you something?"

"Of course. And no need to be so formal here, please, call me Jack."

She turns her head to look directly at him. "Jack. Why did you rescue me from the Dawning? I know not everyone on your crew is happy with what's transpired and I don't want to be the cause for any discord between you and your men."

Jack scratches at the stubble on the side of his left cheek. "Thompson's log. It had his stop at Agrego listed, with the very next destination being Slaver's Bay. Naturally, I thought he was doing Shryke's bidding and we'd find people chained in the hull of the ship, but when I saw his reaction to your little incident with Vane,

I knew something wasn't right."

Lily scoffs playfully. "Little incident?"

Jack clicks his tongue and smirks. "Okay, maybe not so little. Anyway, when you were exposed, my suspicions were confirmed by Thompson's extreme unease. Then, when I saw you, I knew immediately you were the one destined for Slaver's Bay. After you passed out, Thompson admitted everything, sealing the fate of him and his crew."

Lily leans forward on her elbows, the weight of everything that happened settling heavy on her mind.

~

Two nights later, the star-covered sky beckons Lily on deck and she decides to spend some time admiring their brilliance.

The faint sound of music and laughter from the deck greets her when she leaves Jack's quarters. After she pushes open the door to the outer deck, she sees a small group of men gathered together. One strums on a lute while George sings a sea shanty.

As Lily approaches, the song ends and George spots her. He smiles boyishly and waves her over. "Join us."

The men turn to greet her and make space in their little circle.

"Do you sing?" George inquires.

"Afraid it wasn't a talentI was ever able to master."

"Ah, too bad. Well, how about a dance then?" He

stands, holding a hand out to Lily.

"Oh George, I don't know."

"Come on lass," one of the pirates declares, and the others join in.

Lily concedes and joins George in the center of their circle.

"Hastings, give us something lively," George says.

The man with the lute begins strumming again. Lily allows George to put one hand around her waist as she places her right hand in his, then begins following his lead as he starts to spin her. They fall into the groove quickly, moving in a circle that causes the men to take two steps back so there's enough room.

George smiles at Lily who returns it and he stumbles over his feet a little, causing them both to start laughing.

"Roberts, jump in," George calls, and a ginger-haired man steps forward. George spins Lily out and releases her. She twirls right into the waiting arms of Roberts and they continue the dance.

Jack watches from the shadows behind the helm. Lily's laugh carries above the sound of Hastings' lute. It's the first time he's heard her truly laugh, and it's beautiful, musical even. To have gone through what she has and be having a good time like this, her strength was admirable to him.

"Tate, you're up," George calls out. Tate readies himself as Roberts spins Lily to the center of the circle. Roberts steps back while Tate steps in, hooking his elbow with hers. They swing each other around in a small circle as they kick their feet.

Lily realizes that this is the most fun she's had since

before Agrego. She used to have moments like this as a child, but as she got older the focus of her life became all about refinement and preparation for marriage.

"Incredible, isn't it?" Knox asks softly from his spot on the stairs, looking from the scene on the deck below to Jack.

"She is," Jack responds absentmindedly.

Knox chuckles softly.

"I mean…"

"No, she is," Knox agrees, rising then moving to stand next to Jack. He waits a beat. "You care for her."

"Knox, don't," Jack replies, eying his quartermaster.

"She cares for you too."

Jack scoffs. What could she possibly see in someone like him?

Knox smiles knowingly. "I've been watching you both since she awoke."

"Don't be ridiculous. She's a governor's daughter. Her family literally founded the island she lives on."

"So? Ellie's father was a judge; didn't stop her from marrying me."

"That's different."

"I don't think so. Aye, the feeling of love is a deeper level, but it starts with caring for the other person. That young woman down there cares about you, and I don't give a damn what you say, there's a part of you that feels the same. You've learned more about her life in three days than most people would ever deign to. You know the horrors she's been through and you admire her strength; the fact that she's laughing and dancing right now despite it all. If you didn't, we wouldn't be sailing for Molai, we'd be on our way to Mearas to collect a reward and let her family deal with Shryke and their daughter's missing memories."

Knox nudges Jack on the shoulder. "Your father was a bastard, Jack, but you're not. You're nothing like him. The strength within you, the part of you that cares, that comes from your mother, and it's a blessing, not a weakness like he tried to make you believe for so long. Now, take some advice from an older, *wiser* man, and go down there."

Jack sighs, shaking his head slightly as he takes a step forward. "You know *old* man, one of these days I'm gonna…"

A broad smile spreads across Knox's face as Jack makes his way down the steps, not finishing his thought.

"That a boy," Knox whispers after him.

The group parts as Jack steps up. Lily hasn't seen him, but Tate does so he spins her out in Jack's direction. As she looks up to see who's waiting for her, she stumbles when she realizes it's Jack. She's already a little breathless, but now it feels like all the air's been sucked from her lungs.

Jack catches her in a slightly dipped pose, eyes glued to hers. Lily's chest quickly rises and falls as she tries to catch her breath. The immediate sense of safety she feels in Jack's arms comforts her, accompanied by another feeling she can't quite place.

"May I have this dance?" he asks, returning her smile with one of his own, lifting her to a fully upright position.

Lily's eyes light up, which doesn't go unnoticed by

Jack as Knox's words replay in his head.

"You may," she replies softly.

Jack looks over to Hastings, who Lily only just realizes had stopped playing. "Hastings, give us something a little slower, let's allow the lady to catch her breath."

Hastings nods then begins strumming lightly on the chords of the lute.

Jack wraps his right arm behind Lily's waist and takes her right hand in his left. "Is this all right?" he asks as he feels her relax into his hold.

Lily swallows the small lump in her throat and bobs her head twice. At first they just sway a little, but then Jack steps back with his right foot and Lily follows his lead. He guides her around inside the circle made by the men, who might as well not even be there because Jack and Lily are so focused on each other that they see no one and nothing else.

There's a part of Jack's mind that's admonishing him and yelling for him to look away, but there's a bigger, more willful part of him that's enjoying the feel of her body against his, the way she moves in his arms, and the sparkle in her eyes.

The pit of Lily's stomach tenses as she follows Jack's lead. She enjoys the sense of safety in his sturdy arms, the way his palm feels pressed against her spine and the closeness of his body. His eyes are darker than ever in the night and she's willingly drowning in them.

"Who taught you to dance?" she asks, breaking the silence.

"My mother," he replies coolly.

"You're really quite good," Lily continues.

Jack scoffs playfully, which makes Lily laugh.

They fall into a comfortable silence. No additional words are uttered as they gaze at each other, each lost in the depth of the other's eyes. The moment is perfect, nothing exists right now except them and the music. Lily grips Jack's shoulder a little tighter as he pulls her closer, their hearts pounding in their chests as they wonder if the other can hear or feel it.

As their faces slowly draw near, both know what's about to happen and neither does anything to stop it.

Suddenly, their lips meet. It's a gentle kiss, but one laced with an undertone of need. Their bodies have stopped moving to the music as time seems to stand still. Jack wraps both arms around Lily's waist, pulling her in so close there's no longer space between them.

Lily's breath hitches. She'd never been kissed before, but can't imagine one ever being better than this. The sensation of Jack's lips on hers does something to her that's almost indescribable.

Jack finds himself lost in the feel of Lily, the warmth of her soft lips, the way her body effortlessly moulds to his, and the gentle pressure of her arms wrapped around his neck.

He begins to kiss her more deeply, fully realizing that she's returning the energy right back.

Outside of their little bubble, the crew's fallen silent, too surprised to make a sound by attempting to leave, and too intimidated by their Captain to cheer in support of this moment like that would if it were anyone else, so they stay where they are, frozen.

Knox smiles from his spot at the helm. He

remembers when he first met and fell in love with his wife, Ellie, and seeing Jack and Lily like this makes him all the more excited to see her again after these past few months at sea.

The passion between Jack and Lily is escalating as Jack feels his body start to react with excitement and anticipation. Recognition of what's happening to him rips Jack from this beautiful moment and his eyes spring open.

"I can't do this!" his mind screams in frustration.

He quickly breaks their kiss. Lily sways, unsteady from the sudden loss of balance combined with the breathless feeling she's experiencing.

"What? Did I do something wrong?" she asks softly, her eyes full of questions Jack's not ready to answer.

Jack steps back, dropping his hands to his sides. "No, I did," he replies stoically.

Lily takes a purposeful step toward him to close the gap he created, but Jack retreats again.

She presses. "Jack, please, I don't understand."

He hesitates for a moment then quickly turns and starts for the stairs that lead to the stern of the ship. "Forget it." It's a throwaway statement, but Lily hears and follows him.

"Jack, wait. Jack, please. Talk to me. Tell me what…"

Just before his foot hits the first stair, Jack wheels around to face her. His natural height combined with the shadows of the night make him look as imposing as ever. "I said forget it! I'm Captain, my word is final. I do not repeat myself. Know your place on this ship."

The raised tone of his voice surprises Lily and she

stops short. What little she can see of his face and posture in the darkness frightens her. It's the first time she's felt this way since waking up in his quarters.

After everything she'd told him about her life and how she'd been treated the last three years, this is how he's going to react to a kiss of all things? It doesn't make any sense to her.

She straightens her spine, determined to push the fear down, and clears her throat, but does nothing to mask the hurt in her eyes, unsure if he can even see them. "My apologies if I took your instruction to call you Jack for granted, *Captain* Teague. I forgot I'm just a refugee, here only by your good graces, it won't happen again."

Jack inhales deeply, his expression softening, then falling as realization of what he said, and how Lily emphasized 'Captain,' hits him.

As she turns toward the door that ultimately leads to his quarters, he reaches out, grabbing hold of her wrist.

She freezes, immediately trying to fight off memories of when Staunton would grab her by surprise just like this before hurting her.

"Lily…"

"Please, release me, Captain."

She'd stepped into a shadow so he's unable to see her face, but the tremble of her voice is unmistakable, as is the slight shaking he can feel in her arm. He fucked up, and he knows it.

Before he can respond, Lily pulls her wrist from his hand and walks at a steady pace to the door, determined to hold her head high.

Jack hopes for a moment of hesitation on her part so

he knows he'll have a chance to apologize, but it doesn't happen. Lily opens the door, steps through, then lets it slam shut behind her, disappearing from his sight.

She holds it together until she's safely in the confines of Jack's room, but as soon as she shuts the door she sinks to the floor and cries, her head swimming with dastardly memories of Agrego and conflict over what had just happened, versus how their kiss moment before had made her feel.

On deck, Jack rakes his fingers roughly through his hair. *"You're a fuckin' asshole,"* he admonishes himself. He turns and begins climbing the stairs once again when he notices Knox still standing on the deck above.

Knox opens his mouth. "Captain…"

"Not now Knox," Jack replies in a low, calmer voice, then continues up to the stern as images of how his father had treated his mother rush back to him.

Try as he might to be the complete opposite of the cruel bastard his father was, sometimes the damage that man had done slipped out, and in his mind, this was one of those times.

The men left on deck are unsure what to do so they disperse, each with the unspoken understanding that they do not tell anyone what just transpired between their Captain and Lily.

CHAPTER 6
THE WITCH

By early afternoon the following day, Jack and Lily still have not spoken.

Jack hunches at the bow of the ship, knife at the ready as they approach Molai. He's done this so many times before, just a few more minutes until the ship catches the current that will carry his blood into the invisible barrier protecting the island, which will grant them entrance.

Most of the crew's assembled on deck and he keeps looking back in their direction. However, it's not them he's interested in seeing. Lily hasn't emerged from his quarters yet and all he wants is to speak to her, apologize for being a complete asshole, and explain why he pulled back.

Knox was right, he does feel for her, but the reality of their situation, the fact that they come from two very different worlds and that Lily must be returned to hers, hit him in the gut in the middle of that truly amazing kiss. That, coupled with the fact that he'd felt his body responding to the excitement the kiss elicited, he'd panicked in the moment.

While he'd sat at the stern of the ship last night he couldn't help but laugh a little at the fact that someone like him, a man living the life he was and the situations he'd been in, panicked over a kiss. That's when he'd realized he needed to rein in these new feelings, and now all he wanted to do was explain that to Lily.

Just as he's about to turn back around to face the bow, he spots Lily emerging onto the deck. Her steps are tentative and she pauses when their eyes meet. Even from this distance Jack can tell she's nervous as he watches her lace her fingers together and look down.

"Now, Captain!" Tate calls from the helm.

Jack slices the knife across his left palm, and as soon as enough blood pools in his hand he leans over the bow and lets it drip into the sea.

After a few moments, a golden glow appears where the blood fell, then spreads further into the current as it gets carried toward the enchanted barrier ahead of the ship.

Knox looks down over the railing in front of the helm when he sees the fiery red hair he's been waiting for appear on deck. "Lily," he calls warmly.

She turns, angling her head up at him.

"Come, join me, you're going to want to watch this."

Lily nods before making her way up to him. "What's happening?" she asks when she's by his side.

"We're almost there. Jack's opening the path through

the barrier as we speak."

She looks forward to where Jack stands and squints. "I don't see anything."

Knox smiles. "You will."

She nods, but doesn't say another word. While she's excited at the prospect of having her memories restored, she'd be lying if she said she wasn't experiencing any apprehension at the thought of trusting another witch to do it.

"Are you all right?" Knox asks.

Lily keeps her eyes forward. "I'm fine. Why do you ask?"

Knox softens his gaze. "I saw," is all he says in response.

Lily slowly turns her head to face him. "You did?"

He nods.

She sighs. "I don't understand him. What did I do?"

Knox places his hand on the one she has resting on the railing. "You did nothing, my dear. Jack has a reason for everything he does, and while I was also surprised by his reaction last night, I know he regrets it. You have every right to be upset, but please, speak to him, let him explain."

"I tried. He told me to know my place, so if the Captain desires a conversation with me, I await his order to have it."

"Lily…"

"Please, Mr. Knox." She turns back to face the bow and slowly removes her hand from below his.

"Mr. Knox, the Captain will need the salve for his hand," George interjects quietly from his place a few steps behind them.

Knox bows his head once to Lily, then makes his way down the stairs and across the deck.

"Captain, I have the salve," he announces as he approaches Jack, holding it out to him.

Jack turns to him, taking the small glass vial. He chances another quick glance at Lily, who's standing in the same spot at the railing, having a conversation with George.

"How badly did I fuck up last night?" he asks Knox.

"Badly," Knox replies without hesitation. "She thinks she did something wrong, despite my assurance to the contrary, and based on the little she did say, it's clear she's taking ' "know your place' " as an order from Jack Teague, corsair Captain of the Savage Sea, and not Jack Teague, the understanding man you'd been toward her previously."

Jack smooths some of the salve over his palm. "Fuck," he exclaims in a low voice. "I regretted it the moment I fuckin' said it. I can't believe I got in my own head so deeply and so quickly."

"You need to talk to her, and fast. She awaits your order to do so."

Jack's brow furrows. "Awaits my order?"

Knox nods once. "That's what she said."

"Damn it. You're right, I need to fix this. Thank you, Knox."

Knox begins to back away but stops. He needs Jack to hear what he has to say, regardless of how he may react. "Captain?"

Jack corks the vial of salve. "Yes, Knox?"

"You are not your father, remember that."

Knox departs quickly before Jack can respond, hoping the young man will finally believe that truth.

~

"How much longer?" Lily asks George.

"Should be any moment now," he replies.

As if on cue, the open air in front of the Savage Sea starts to shimmer and Lily gasps as the ship passes through the barrier.

Once on the other side, she's enamored by the breathtaking island now floating a short distance away. "Oh my," she whispers with surprise.

"I know. I've been several times since I joined the crew and I always have the same reaction."

From what she can see, the beach is a mix of black and white sand, branching in separate but equal directions from a center point where what appears to be a small river flows out of the jungle behind the beach.

"Black and white sand?" she wonders aloud.

"Balance, remember?" The reply comes from Jack, who now stands on the deck below her.

Lily looks down at him, surprised by how quickly he made it back from the bow without her noticing. "Oh, yes. Thank you, Captain." She looks back to the island, eyes following the stretch of the lush green mountain range that rises behind the jungle.

"Lily..."

"Captain?"

He hesitates before deciding against furthering the conversation right now. They're approaching their anchor point and need to prepare themselves to disembark. The crew's also too close for comfort for him to say what he needs to. Instead, he turns his attention to George.

"Ready the longboats," Jack instructs.

"Aye, Captain," George replies before departing Lily's side.

Jack spins slowly to face the crew assembled on deck. "Turner, take some men and prepare to load two kegs of gunpowder, the herbs we've acquired, and our empty vials into one of the boats, then have them begin rowing for the shore."

Turner nods, taps the back of his hand against the three closest crew members and they make their way below deck.

"Mr. Knox, I leave it to you to divide up the rest of the crew for ship inspection, repairs, et cetera."

"Of course, Captain. All will be ready upon your return tomorrow."

Jack then faces Lily, who hasn't moved from her spot. "Let's prepare to head ashore. Once we get to the beach it'll take a few hours to hike through the jungle to reach Eudora. Hopefully we'll get there around sunset, maybe slightly after."

Lily descends the stairs to Jack's level so she can retrieve a canteen and some food for the journey from the galley. As she passes Jack he moves his hand ever so slightly so as to allow their fingers to brush against each other. It gives her pause and she glances at him. She finds softened features looking back at her, Jack's eyes full of regret.

Lily blinks but stays silent, then continues below deck a moment later. The conversation she knows his expression was telling her they need to have will have to wait.

Jack sighs after she departs before heading to his quarters to pack a few items and grab his tricorn.

~

As the two longboats approach the shore, Lily's eyes dart around the surrounding jungle. Her heart thunders as uncertainty and anxiety rise within her.

Once they're in shallow enough water, Jack and Turner jump from their longboat while Hastings, George and two other members of the crew jump from the other. All of them grab some ropes and pull the boats up onto the sand and out of the water.

Jack approaches the side of the boat when they've finished as Turner drives a stake into the sand with the rope wrapped around it.

"Let me help you out of there," he offers softly, holding out his hand.

Lily hesitates for a moment then takes it. She jumps from the side and as her feet sink into the soft sand, Jack steadies her. After so many days on the water her legs feel a little wobbly.

"Don't worry, your body will adjust to being back on land quickly," he assures her.

Lily looks at him as she goes to take a step and her right knee gives out slightly.

Jack drops her hand and places both of his on either side of her waist, exerting light but firm pressure to keep her standing. "Are you all right?"

She nods.

Neither of them attempt to separate.

Jack keeps his voice low. "I am so sorry. I never should've said what I did last night. I promise I'll explain when we have a moment to ourselves, but until then, please just know it was nothing you did, it was all me."

Lily sees Turner and the others approach over Jack's shoulder so she simply nods and says, "thank you."

"Captain, we're ready to begin," Turner announces.

Jack reluctantly releases Lily's waist before stepping back and turning to his crew. Hastings and Drake each have a keg of gunpowder fastened to their backs while the others share the remainder of the items they've brought as gifts for Eudora.

"All right, let's go," he replies.

Lily moves behind Jack while the others file into line behind them and they begin following the river into the jungle.

Despite her dress, Lily's able to keep up with their pace. She'd assumed the kegs of gunpowder would be difficult to carry, but it's clear they've done this before as she watches Hastings and Drake navigate the uneven landscape. When they come to a rock formation that requires more finesse, they remove the kegs from their backs and the group works together to lift them up each level of rock.

"What does a witch need with gunpowder?" she asks Jack during one of their rests.

He takes a swig from his canteen. "Well, our crew isn't the only one with permission to see Eudora. She may be a bestower of gifts, but she also likes to trade."

"Gunpowder's of high value for sailors."

"Exactly."

"Is there anything I really need to know before I meet Eudora? Anything I should or shouldn't say?"

Jack smiles. Lily hates what that smile does to her right now. Her anger over last night has ebbed, but there's still a sense of hurt, even after his brief but sincere apology on the beach.

"Just be honest, she appreciates that. Besides, if you lie she'll know. She'll be going into your head after all."

Lily's expression falls slightly. "Right." She inserts the cork back in her canteen then turns away slightly.

Jack notices the change on her face and moves until he's crouching in front of her. "Hey, hey, look at me. Eudora's nothing like the witch who did this to you. And, I'll be there the entire time, I won't let anything bad happen to you. Trust me."

Lily takes a deep breath and nods. "I do."

"That's a good little flower," he jokes.

"Would you stop with that?" she replies with feigned exasperation.

"Never," Jack whispers with a wicked grin.

"We ready?" Turner asks the group.

Everyone rises, gathers their things, and they continue on.

The sun has just about set as they make their final push and crest the hill that leads to Eudora's little hut.

"Wait here," Jack instructs everyone before he makes his way to the hut's front steps.

Lily takes in the sight of the hut from her spot along the treeline. It looks cozy, with its thatched roof covered in moss, and small porch.

Before Jack can lift his foot to climb the two steps, the door opens. Eudora steps over the threshold and onto the porch.

"I've been waiting for you, Captain Teague."

~

Eudora slowly circles Lily while Jack watches intensely, arms crossed over his chest.

Lily had assumed what Eudora would look like based solely on the witch she'd already encountered, but she was extremely mistaken.

Eudora appeared to be about her mother's age. She has fawny, beige skin with what appears to be a slight pink undertone, which is brought out by a head of perfectly straight hair that is equal parts black and white.

Her almond-shaped eyes contain the same balance of color, one with a black pupil and white iris that was a shade darker than her sclera, the other a white pupil with a black iris.

Lily's still a ball of nerves, but there is something about being in Eudora's presence that comforts her.

"Yes," Eudora murmurs while evaluating Lily, stopping in front of her. "I sense its essence," she continues, her eyes finally meeting Lily's, and pointing her finger at Lily's forehead.

"I can see the scar the magic left behind. The spell used on you was a powerful one, excruciatingly painful for you to experience, I am sure."

Lily closes her eyes and shudders, the memory of that night rushing back to her. She can barely nod in agreement.

Eudora shakes her head slowly. "I thought so. 'Tis a shame so many of my sisters have begun using their gifts to harm. We were never meant to be that way, our magic is supposed to be for the greater good, protectors of the world we watch over, maintain the balance. But, as with so many things in life, even the most pure of intentions can be corrupted and destroyed by the influence of man."

She keeps her eyes focused on Lily, but addresses Jack. "What is it you're looking for, Captain Teague?"

Jack remains motionless. "A way to help her before she returns home."

"Mm, you want to retrieve her memories."

"Yes."

She turns to Jack now, her eyes bearing down on him. "There are some things my magic I cannot do…"

Lily places her hand over her heart and looks up to the sky. She knew she shouldn't have let herself hope.

Eudora softens her gaze, having seen Lily's change in

demeanor. "This is not one of them. The question is, are you prepared for what you might learn?"

"I'll do anything. I need to remember, no matter what comes back to me."

"All right. Give me your hands."

Lily raises her arms and Eudora takes a firm hold of both hands, each in one of her own.

"Do not be frightened." No sooner has she closed her eyes than a jolt of energy passes from her hands into Lily's, causing Lily to wobble.

"I see it!" she exclaims, releasing Lily's hands. "There is dark magic floating in your head. I can pull it out, but it will only restore your experiences, not answer any questions beyond that which you've been part of. Do you understand? You might end up with more questions than answers, and depending on those questions, you may have no choice but to get those answers from the ones responsible for this atrocity."

Lily gasps, pulling her hands out of Eudora's grasp.

Jack steps closer to the two of them, his mouth slightly ajar. "There has to be another way."

"Unless Lily's parents know why she was taken, there is not. You must face your demon, Lily Mearas, and triumph over him." She pauses briefly before turning and walking back toward the door. "Follow me."

Jack and Lily spare a glance at each other. She holds out her hand and Jack slips his fingers between hers before guiding her up the steps and into the hut, followed by George while Turner, Hastings and Drake carry the remaining items and kegs for Eudora around the side of the hut.

When she steps over the threshold, Lily looks around. Despite the heavier air outside, the inside is cool, with an immediate feeling of coziness to it.

A small bed sits next to a window looking out into the jungle behind in the back right corner. Immediately to the right of the door is a tall square table with a wash basin sitting in the middle. Pieces of clothing hang off the wall directly behind it with what appear to be hooks carved from tree bark.

Lily's eyes follow Eudora's path as she crosses to the back left corner of the room, passing a small, circular table low to the floor, covered in a sheer white cloth and a black bowl that looks like a combination of a mini cauldron and a stew pot. Once Eudora's behind the table she begins assessing the semi-circular shelves built into the corner of the room.

"George, you can place the herbs and things you've brought on the table next to the rocking chair, then leave us, please," she instructs in a pleasant but matter of fact tone.

George clears his throat. "Yes, ma'am." He then takes a few steps over to the table, lays out the herbs, empty vials, bits of fabric, and small cookware. When he's done, he nods to Jack then exits the hut in search of the others, who he knows are likely resting down by the stream a few yards from here.

Once George departs, Eudora begins pulling bottles from the shelves, cradling them in her left arm as she continues. After gathering what she needs, she approaches the circular table, gets down on her knees, then pours each into the large black bowl. A thin spiral

97

of smoke swirls from the bowl as the contents are emptied into it.

Lily looks tentatively at Jack and he at her.

"What are you doing?" he inquires.

"This will allow the magic to be pulled from Lily's mind and bring her memories back."

Eudora empties the final vial into the bowl then lowers herself into a cross-legged position on the floor. She raises her arms, palms up, and begins chanting. Lily recognizes it as the same language the witch responsible for the dark magic in her head spoke three years ago. Eudora closes her eyes as the volume of her voice lowers before entering what seems to be a meditative state.

Jack and Lily sit opposite Eudora and stare as the room appears to get darker for the briefest of moments. They take a final look at one another as their eyelids close, and their minds begin to wander.

When Lily opens her eyes she's standing, surrounded by a light mist of varying shades of pink. It's slightly disorienting to her and she rubs her eyes. The silhouette of a person approaches through the mist. As it does, Lily hears her name being called out.

Suddenly, Jack appears. "What is this place?" he wonders out loud once he spots Lily.

Lily shrugs, still looking around, but there's nothing here besides the mist.

Eudora materializes before them. "You are in a higher realm of consciousness. Your minds are linked, which controls this entire space." With a wave of her hand a section of mist clears and all three of them look at their bodies, seemingly asleep on the hut's floor.

"In order to reverse the magic, you must retrace your steps, so to speak. Start with the last thing you remember before Agrego. Once you do, the spell will start to unravel and your memories will return. As I said before, you may not like what you see, but if you want answers, it's necessary."

She turns to Jack. "And for you to understand what you're getting into by choosing to help her, you too have to see where Lily's been. Observe, see if you notice anything in her memories that can help you."

"No," Lily gasps.

"You must," Eudora replies, giving her a sympathetic look.

Jack can see the fear growing in Lily. "I want to understand."

"Jack..." Lily can't find the right words, so she sighs, letting her shoulders slump as she turns to Eudora, fully aware there's no other way. "How do I do this?"

"Focus on the beach on Mearas. Don't try to force anything, just let it come to you. Once you do, the spell will start to unravel. Let your mind guide you. I will pull you back to reality when the time comes."

Eudora evaporates into the mist, leaving Jack and Lily alone.

With a shaky breath Lily closes her eyes and thinks back to the day she disappeared from the world she'd known.

~

When she opens her eyes, she's standing in the sand on the beach on Mearas. Immediately, her eyes fall on herself, standing by the shoreline, looking out at the water.

"Whoa," she exclaims in a low voice.

Jack steps into her field of vision. He looks around, taking in the scenery. "This is a beautiful beach."

"Yeah, it was my favorite spot on Mearas. So peaceful and quiet, rarely anyone around; a perfect place to just get away and think."

"I can see that." His voice is soft as he takes in the place Lily had once sought solace and found peace.

They approach past Lily. As they reach her she bends down and picks up a small shell, washes the sand off, then straightens. No sooner does she stand up then a hand appears in front of her face. She screams but it's quickly muffled when the hand presses a cloth against her nose and mouth.

Both Jack and Lily take a quick step backward.

"I don't understand," she remarks with confusion as past Lily struggles in the invisible grip she appears to be in. "I don't see anything."

Jack thinks for a moment, then it clicks. "Eudora said we'd only experience what you did, right?"

Lily nods.

"You must not have seen who took you," he replies, concern evident in his tone.

They both watch as past Lily's body begins to slump, her eyes closing as she does.

"No, no, no," Lily whispers, her voice slightly hoarse with suppressed emotion.

Jack's about to pull her to him when they hear disembodied voices.

"She's out. Hurry up, let's get back to the ship and get the hell out of here," one says.

"We'll stick to the treeline, but put this blanket over her just in case," another responds.

Lily startles as realization hits. "My experiences," she repeats. "I understand now. I may not be conscious but I can still hear at this point. Perhaps not all hope is lost after all."

Lily thinks about the moment her body slumped, and she and Jack watch as time seems to rewind to that moment. This time, instead of focusing on what's happening visually, they pay attention to the voices.

"I don't recognize the first man, but the second is definitely Staunton," she announces with confidence. "I'd know his disgusting voice anywhere."

As the visual of Lily's slumped body fades, Jack and Lily follow the sound of the disembodied voices as they trek across the sand back to the treeline.

"Well, well, looks like someone couldn't help himself. Do you think she saw?" one of the voices asks, clearly pointing out another person Lily and Jack can't see.

"I have no fucking idea, but I'll deal with him. Keep heading for the ship and get ready to set sail, I'll be right behind you," Staunton replies.

The voices start to fade. The last thing Jack and Lily hear is Staunton ask the unknown man, "What the hell are you doing here?"

Jack and Lily gaze at the empty space. Lily's heart drops. Someone watched her get taken, and did nothing about it.

Lily sinks to the sand, her breathing uneven and rapid. She clutches at her chest as Jack kneels in front of her. She looks up at him, tears welling in her eyes.

"Someone saw! I... can't... Jack..." Her breathing is so erratic and her mind's racing, she can't seem to form a coherent thought.

"Hey, hey," he replies in a calm voice, picking up her hand. "Focus on me, and only on me." Jack places the palm of her hand on his chest, directly over his heart so she can feel its steady beat. "Breathe in," he continues, then takes a slow, steady breath so Lily has something to mimic.

She follows Jack's lead, eyes glued to him. Her tears fall slowly but she doesn't try to wipe them away, she's focused only on breathing the same way he is. After a few deep breaths she can feel her heart start to calm.

As Jack watches her breathing return to normal, he slowly reaches over and gently wipes the tears from her eyes, then places his palm against her warm cheek, keeping it there as her head tilts slightly to rest in it.

"You're all right," he reassures softly.

Lily lifts her free hand and holds it against the one Jack has pressed to her cheek. "Thank you," she replies, her soul relishing the comfort of his touch.

Before either can say another word, the pink mist returns and swirls around them. When it lifts they're in their same positions but in the hull of a ship.

Jack rises slowly then holds out his hand to help Lily

up. When she's standing they start to look around.

"Hey!" a voice screams from behind them.

They turn to find past Lily locked in the brig, her hands wrapped around the bars. She pulls at them while she screams "Someone! Anyone! Why am I here?" The raspy sound of her voice tells them she's been screaming for a while.

Both Jack and Lily spin around slowly, taking in the hull. There's no one down here besides her.

Lily looks at the version of herself within the cell. Her face and hands are dirty, and her hair's a bit of a mess. "I've been in here a while," she observes.

Jack nods. "If they sailed straight for Agrego from Mearas, I'm betting you're almost there."

The sound of footsteps on the stairs leading up to the deck draws their attention. Past Lily calls out, then gasps as Staunton comes into view. She retreats from the cell bars.

Staunton slowly approaches, like a hunter stalking his prey. When he reaches the cell door he takes a key from his breast pocket, unlocks the door then steps through after he pulls it open.

Past Lily backs up into the wooden wall that forms one side of the ship's hull as Staunton approaches.

"What are you doing? Why did you take me?" she asks shakily.

"Sh, sh," he replies, lifting his right hand then using it to brush a section of loose hair from Lily's face, tucking it behind her ear. "All in good time."

Jack tenses as he watches Staunton's gaze pass over the tops of Lily's breasts before licking his lips. Both past and present Lily notice as well and freeze for different reasons; past is afraid of what he might do, present is fearful of what he ultimately does do.

The anger within Jack reaches a boiling point and he lunges forward to tackle Staunton. He passes right through him though, as if he were a ghost, and stops himself before he crashes into the cell bars. He mutters "Shit," under his breath before returning to full height and turning back to reluctantly watch the rest of the scene unfold.

"Please," past Lily begs.

"Please, please, it's always please," Staunton mocks in response before stepping back and exiting the cell. "For as privileged and educated as you are, you need to learn patience." He locks the door as Lily rushes to it.

"Patience? You want me to be patient as a prisoner in the hull of a ship with no idea why I'm here?" Her voice is raised in response.

"Afraid you have no other choice." Staunton grins mischievously. "Don't worry, we're almost there. If you really want to know why, you'll have to ask *him* at some point... that is, if you ever make it back to Mearas." He turns away from the cell then heads for the stairs.

Past Lily grips the cell bars. "Who's *him*?" she demands. "Who are you talking about?!"

Staunton departs, leaving her lost in a fog of confusion. She eventually moves away from the bars and takes a seat on the floor, her back pressed against the hull wall. "Who's he?" she mutters to herself.

Jack and present Lily watch as past Lily slowly knocks her head against the wall lightly.

"That's the second time we've heard reference to a *he*," Jack announces.

"And I still have no idea who that is," Lily replies. "Do you think they wiped my memory of these moments in case I started to really think through all the possibilities of who it could be?"

"It's possible." Jack scratches at his stubble.

The pink mist swirls again and they're suddenly in the room within Agrego's fort where Lily encountered the witch.

"Oh no," present Lily exclaims as they stare from the shadows at past Lily strapped to the table.

Jack pulls her into his side, wrapping one arm around her waist. "It's all right, you're safe now. Don't watch this." His voice is warm and full of care.

Lily nods, sinks into his side some more then closes her eyes. She remembers this encounter but there must be something that happened here Shryke wanted her to forget.

As the memory unfolds, Jack struggles to maintain his composure. Everything happens exactly the way Lily had described on the Savage Sea, and just when he starts to question what could possibly have been erased from her memory, Jack gets his answer when Shryke approaches the table.

While Shryke glares down at Lily, he makes an observation. "You look so much like your mother."

The Lily on the table widens her eyes at him. "What?" she gasps.

The Lily in Jack's arms pops her eyes open. "What did he just say?"

105

"He said you look like your mother."

"Shryke knew my mother?" The surprise in her voice is unmistakable.

"Did your parents never mention him?"

"Not once. I'm sure father either knew him or at least of him, given his position, but mother? She never said a word."

Shyrke looks to the witch as she brings the potion over to the table. "Make her forget what I just said too," he instructs.

The witch nods once then tells him how he needs to help her get Lily to swallow the liquid.

Present Lily's shoulders start to shake as the pink mist swirls around them again. When her eyes open she's laying on the floor of Eudora's hut.

Lily and Jack slowly rise to their feet.

The sadness in her eyes breaks his heart. He goes to reach for her, but Lily turns and runs out to the little front porch.

Jack starts to follow when Eudora holds her arm out in front of him.

"She needs time to process this, alone," Eudora states.

CHAPTER 7
SCARS & PROMISES

Lily stands on the hut's porch, her hands gripping the wooden railing, knuckles white. She doesn't know what's worse, the memories themselves or now knowing someone on Mearas knew she'd been taken by Staunton and Shryke somehow knew her mother.

Her head's spinning with more questions than answers at this point.

Eudora steps up next to her, a cup of tea in one hand. "Here, drink this," she says softly. "I'm sorry for the pain, but it was the only way to undo the magic."

Lily takes the cup from her. "I know." She sighs, turning to face Eudora and leaning against the railing. "It's just, I still don't know why I was taken. There was nothing they made me forget that answers that question, just some vague reference '*he*' and '*him*'. And, while I now know Shryke and my mother have some sort of connection, I don't know what that is. Did they grow up together? Did they meet once at a ball and he just remembers what she looks like? I still feel so lost."

"I fear the first is something only Shryke can answer,

and your mother the second part, once you return to Mearas."

Lily sighs and takes a sip of tea. "I was afraid of that." She turns to face the stream again, her eyes falling on the sleeping Savage Sea crew.

Eudora continues. "You know, if you follow this path to the left, you'll find your way to the waterfall that powers this stream. There's a deep pool of water at its base. Why don't you go take a dip and clear your mind? You've been on the sea for days, I'm sure it would do you good to rinse off as well."

Lily offers a small smile. "A swim in fresh water does sound divine." She hands the cup back to Eudora and steps down onto the path. "Just this way?" she asks, pointing to a worn trail that wraps around the hut.

"Yes, it's not too far, you can't miss it."

Eudora watches Lily depart.

As Lily walks the path illuminated by bright moonlight streaming through the treetops, she listens to the calming sounds of her surroundings, especially the babbling stream. She feels oddly at peace here and takes a few deep breaths to enjoy the fragrance of the flowers around her.

A short distance ahead, the path opens into a large clearing. The gorgeous pool of crystal blue water in front of her is being filled by a 20 foot high waterfall, just as Eudora described.

"Beautiful," she whispers, staring at it.

Lily approaches the edge of the pool. Without a cloud in the sky, the moon illuminates the pool of water, revealing just how deep it is.

She bends down, her hand skimming over the top of the water. It's tepid, absolutely perfect for what she needs.

Lily reaches behind her back to undo the lacing of the dress. She kicks off her shoes as she does and works to loosen the dress as much as possible. Once she gets it to a point where she can move more freely, she grabs the hem of the dress, lifts it over her head, and shimmies her way out of it. Her chemise follows right after.

She jumps from the edge as far into the water as she can. A slight chill washes over her as she sinks below the surface, but it feels so good.

When her body stops sinking, Lily kicks for the surface and breaks through. She moves her legs to keep herself afloat as she wipes the water from her face and runs her fingers through her hair.

"This feels amazing," she thinks to herself while looking up at the sky. The full moon's brightness draws her in, pulling a relaxed smile from her face. Despite everything that just happened, she focuses only on this moment as she begins running her hands over her body to rid it of the dirt and sweat that's accumulated since escaping Agrego.

Lily floats around in the water for a bit, studying the waterfall and the uneven rock wall it flows over. Suddenly, it becomes clear to her that there's a pathway to the top. She climbs out of the water, pulls her chemise back on over her head, then approaches the wall.

As she navigates her way up the wall, excitement builds in her stomach. She's never done anything like this before and she can't help but think how mortified her parents would be to see their daughter in a chemise, climbing a wall. Imaging the looks on their faces makes her smile.

When she makes it to the top of the wall she quickly looks down over the side, pride in her accomplishment rising within her.

Lily steps back from the edge then approaches the side of the waterfall. The water doesn't look like it's moving too fast but after a quick assessment she decides that jumping from the outer edge would be safer. "It's only 20 feet," she repeats to herself over and over.

Jack emerges from the treeline while Lily's making her assessment. He'd waited as long as he could but it was getting unbearable, he needed to find and speak to Lily, so while Eudora busied herself with organizing the herbs they'd brought, he set out along the path to look for Lily.

He calls her name just as his eyes fall on her discarded dress and shoes. Suddenly, something splashes into the water and his head snaps up. Panic explodes inside him as he looks from the waterfall to the spot on the water where the ripples from whatever entered it continue to expand.

Jack unhooks his pistol, sword and dagger in an instant then takes a running dive into the water.

Lily feels something grip her wrist tightly. She's no longer sinking toward the bottom of the pool of water, but instead is being pulled upward. When her head breaks through the surface she takes a deep breath. She's barely gotten her bearings when Jack starts.

"What the hell were you thinking?" he demands.

"What?" She clears her eyes of water with her free hand and looks at him, confused by the entire scenario. He's a mix of anger and horror. "Jack…"

Jack holds her wrist tighter as he kicks to keep them both treading water. "Lily, I know you're in pain but…"

"Jack!" Her sharp tone silences him as she pulls her wrist from his grip, immediately aware why he looks so concerned. "Jack, did you not notice how deep the pool is? The waterfall's *maybe* 20 feet high. I wanted to do something that would let me feel free and thought the jump would be exciting!" She smiles broadly at him.

He looks stunned. "So, you did it on purpose but for fun?"

"Yes," she laughs.

Jack wipes away the water dripping down his face. He doesn't know what to say now. He'd thought the worst but Lily had just done something he had so many times when he was growing up.

Lily splashes water at him and nods up at the waterfall, her smile transitioning into a playful grin. "Come on."

She turns away from him, then swims to the water's edge, Jack following right behind her.

He watches as she climbs out and he can't help but trace the lines of her body as the chemise she wears clings to her wet skin. He wants her more than he'd ever admit aloud. *"I'm in so much fucking trouble,"* he thinks as he forces himself to look away and hoist himself out of the water.

Lily notices the way his soaked shirt drapes over Jack's muscled arms, moulding around his back and abdomen.

He's beautiful. She wants to be wrapped in those strong arms of his again. The kiss they shared on deck fills her mind, but a pang of disappointment quickly follows at his reaction immediately after. She does her best to push it all away, but his soaked body makes it extremely difficult.

She giggles when she sees Jack's feet. "You kept your boots on?"

He looks down and can't help but laugh. The only things he'd discarded before jumping into the water were his pistol, dagger and sword, which now lay next to Lily's green dress.

"You may want to take those off now before we jump. Wouldn't want them to fill with water and you end up drowning on me, now would we, Captain?" she asks, putting a playful emphasis on Captain.

Jack grins as he starts kicking off his boots. "Oh, it would take more than water-logged boots to drown me, little flower."

Her heart skips a beat. Lily liked it when he called her that. "Good to know, Captain," she chortles.

Jack snorts at her repeated use of Captain as his second boot falls to the ground. "Are you a pirate now?"

Lily turns toward the rock path and wall leading up to the waterfall and begins walking. "Would you like it if I was?"

Jack pauses before following. *It would certainly make things a hell of a lot easier,* he thinks in reply.

Lily registers his silence and stops climbing, the smile fading from her face. She slowly turns to him. "Well?"

she asks softly.

"Lily, please."

"No, answer me."

Jack sighs. "This is no life for a woman like you," he begins, realizing the conversation he'd been avoiding is about to happen, whether he likes it or not.

Lily narrows her eyes at him. "A woman like me?"

"You're a governor's daughter, a woman of society. You…"

She lets out an exasperated sound and spins back around, starting the climb again. "Would you stop with that? Who I was born to does not define who I am. The life I'd been raised for is not what I envision for myself anymore; a gentle, submissive woman married off to some titled man to bear his children and be seen and not heard. I mean, we had this conversation already. Did you think I wasn't being sincere?"

Jack scrambles slightly to keep up with her.

"I am not the naive woman who was taught those things. The last three years have been absolute hell. They've made me defiant, strong-willed, determined. I've been a prisoner, beaten for unjustifiable reasons, and made to feel like I was nothing. You literally just saw a small glimpse into it, and what you saw barely scratched the surface. I went from a gilded cage to a hellish prison and I don't want to go back to either. I want freedom."

Lily makes it to the top of the wall and steps aside for Jack to be able to finish his ascent. "I know I have to go home. I have to see my parents and figure out what they know about Shryke, but I don't want to stay there. I'm not the daughter they remember and I want to live a life of my choosing, Jack."

When Jack reaches the top, he brushes off his hands as he stands, then stares into her blazing eyes.

"To love and be loved without conditions. Jack, I..." Lily steps onto a patch of grass bathed in bright moonlight. She gestures to herself. "I'm physically and emotionally scarred in ways that will never be acceptable to the members of the society I was raised in. I mean, fuck them and their absurd way of thinking, but it's just how that part of society is. A woman should be pure, angelic, in all ways..."

Jack's surprised by her curse but to hear her speak so freely is mesmerizing. "Lily, we all have scars."

She shakes her head. "Not like these, and certainly not in high society."

Jack's jaw drops open slightly as the woman before him unties her chemise and lets it fall down around her arms. The moonlight illuminates her body as she slowly turns so her back is fully exposed to him. She shows him the extent of her wounds, of which there are so many more than he'd expected. Almost her entire back is covered in scars, and although he'd been privy to her memories, she hadn't shown him the beatings, so he had no idea the scars were this numerous.

Lily continues to turn slowly until she's facing him again. "I'll have these forever," she concludes, eyes now misty and distant.

He can't take it anymore, he needs to rid her of this pain and dispel the belief she holds that these scars now define her.

Before Lily can utter another word, Jack closes the distance between them in two strides, takes her head in one hand and wraps the other around the small of her back, then pulls her into him as his mouth crashes onto hers, kissing her deeply.

Lily melts into him, returning his passion, just as she had when they danced.

This time though, she can't help but notice there's more of a fervor to the way his mouth possesses hers.

Jack laces his fingers through her hair, pulling back gently, which forces their lips to part and Lily to look up at him. "You're beautiful, inside and out, Lily Mearas. Never let anyone make you feel otherwise. You are absolutely perfect."

Jack releases Lily's hair and takes a step back. He grabs hold of the lower hem of his shirt and lifts it over his head, discarding it on the ground.

Lily's eyes roam every inch of his exposed skin, taking in the scars; one is long and thin across Jack's lower abdomen, there is a circular one below his left shoulder, which looks like a bullet hole, two slashes on the inside of his right forearm, and a bumpy one that crosses diagonally over his heart. He turns slowly to show her the three on his back, the exit wound of the bullet, and one jagged slash that curves over the top of his left bicep, courtesy of his father.

Lily moves toward him. Jack lifts her left hand and guides her fingers over each scar slowly, detailing how they came to be.

"Your father did this?" she asks, her fingers paused over his bicep.

"First scar I ever received. I was twelve."

"Why would he do this?"

Jack hesitates, but ultimately decides she needs to know. She'd been honest with him, and it was time for him to do the same. "My father was not a good man. All those stories people like to tell about pirates, you know, the ones about indiscriminate pillaging, raping and killing? Well, my father was one of those types of pirates. He was a nasty drunk too. One night, he came back from a voyage absolutely pissed out of his mind and immediately began laying into my mother. I couldn't stand for it anymore so I charged at him, just to get him off her. And I succeeded. But, I did it with too much speed and fell on top of him. Before I could even really begin to get up, he grabbed hold of my arm and slashed at it with his dagger."

Lily looks from Jack to his scar while listening to his story.

"After that, he got up and stormed out. Mother patched me up and kept telling me everything would be all right, but I had this sinking feeling that I'd made a terrible mistake. The next morning, my father returned, pulled me out of bed and said that if I thought I was ready to be a tough man, it was time to prove it."

Jack closes his eyes and pauses for a moment before continuing. "Despite my mother's pleas for him not to do it, that I was too young, he dragged me down to the docks and onto the Savage Sea."

"That's the day you became a pirate?"

Jack smiles tentatively "Sort of. That's the day I entered the world of piracy, but to become a true pirate, well, that doesn't happen until after your first kill."

"And when did that happen?"

"When I was 16. You see, I was finally able to return home a year after I was brought aboard. When I got there though, I found out my mother had been killed shortly after I'd left. A fight had broken out at the tavern she'd taken a job at as a barmaid and she was shot."

"Oh Jack, I'm so sorry."

"My father was unphased by her death. I, however, blamed him for it. Had he not taken me away, I would've been the one working somewhere and she never would've needed to take that job. I made a promise to myself that my father would pay for everything he'd ever done that wronged my mother, me or anyone else. I got back on the ship and for the next three years, Vane and I trained every day."

"One day, my father said something about my mother and I saw red. I challenged him. He accepted, thinking he'd kick my ass like so many times before, but this," Jack says while bringing Lily's hand up to the scar across his heart. "This is the final mark he made on my body. I took every bit of Vane's training and unleashed all my anger on my father. His blade may have crossed my chest, but mine slit his throat. He was my first kill, the one that officially made me a pirate."

Lily gently rests her cheek against Jack's chest, her fingers still poised on the scar.

He wraps his arms around her, holding her as close as he can, then lets his chin relax onto the top of her head, thinking about how right it feels to be wrapped around her while actively trying to push away all the uncertainty and danger of any sort of future together.

Jack's surprised when Lily presses her lips to the scar over his heart, and his breath catches in his throat.

Her name slips through his teeth like a whisper on the wind, but she hears it, and it excites her.

When she looks up at Jack again she watches as his eyes darken. It's clear now that he wants her just as much as she wants him. She keeps her hand atop the scar over his heart and lifts the other so it rests on the side of his jaw. "I see you, Jack Teague, and I'm not afraid. Please, tell me you feel the same, tell me you're willing to take the risk, because I've fallen for you, and the thought of returning to Mearas without knowing for certain that you'll be by my side to face whatever awaits us, is unbearable."

Jack exhales shakily. Between her openness earlier and now this, it was what he needed to hear to win his internal battle over wanting to be with her, regardless of their circumstances. She's right, they will figure it out and they'll face the world together.

"It may be scarred, but you have my whole heart, Lily Mearas."

He slips his arms around Lily, lifting her fully into his embrace as she wraps her legs around his waist. He kisses her fervently, finally releasing all his turmoil and surrenders himself to her. When his mouth isn't pressed to hers it's delivering hunger-laced kisses from her neck down to just above her bosom.

The surprised moan that escapes her lips causes his pulse and desire to quicken. With Lily still wrapped around him, Jack lowers them to the plushy grass until Lily's back rests on the ground, and he is perched above her.

Lily's chest heaves below the loose chemise. The excitement she felt in the pit of her stomach travels to between her legs. It was a strange yet thrilling sensation she'd never experienced before.

She feels the pressure of Jack's hips against her own. "I don't know what to…" she begins.

"It's ok," Jack replies with a soft smile. "I'll take care of you."

His left hand hovers above her hips. "Do you trust me?"

Lily nods, the anticipation continuing to build within her.

Jack adjusts his positioning so his face is directly above hers. The corner of his mouth turns up at the thought of her body being his at any moment, before he begins kissing Lily again.

He can't help thinking that the start of a life for himself he'd never truly envisioned, with a woman he still felt he didn't deserve, was about to begin. But, she was his just as much as he was hers. That is all that matters to him at this very moment, and he needs to hear it again.

"Say it again," he urges.

Lily smiles, making eye contact with him and whispers, "I'm yours Jack Teague, from now until the end of my days."

That's all he has to hear to push him over the edge. Jack slides his left hand between her thighs and grins against her mouth when Lily's eyes widen and a gasp comes through her parted lips.

~

The sun crests over the mountains, its light shining directly on Lily's face as she lays curled up on the ground, Jack's long arms holding her close. Its brightness causes her to stir as she slowly blinks the sleep from her eyes.

While her gaze flickers to the long died out embers of the small fire Jack had created to keep them warm, she breathes deeply. For the first time in three years, she feels rested.

She smiles when she feels the steady rise and fall of Jack's chest against her back, his warm breath blowing onto her shoulder.

Lily's careful not to move too much so as not to disturb him, but she's able to bring one of her hands up to her lips. She passes her fingertips over them and smirks as the memory of last night fills her. In his passion, Jack had bit down on her lower lip several times so she figured that was the cause for their slight swollenness this morning.

As their time together replays in her mind, she makes a mental note of how she feels in this moment. Much of her body is stiff, and there's a dull throb between her legs, but she also still has some of the euphoric sensations she'd experienced last night. Those are the ones she focuses on, and the more she does, the more she feels the heat build within her until she involuntarily clenches her thighs together.

The soft chuckle in her ear startles Lily. She rolls over to find Jack awake and gazing at her. When she's fully facing him he wraps his arms around her again and drapes his leg over hers, essentially cocooning her in.

"What are you laughing about?" Lily asks playfully.

"Thinking about last night, were you?"

Lily furrows her brow. "How'd you know?"

Jack grins. "I've been awake, just didn't want to disturb you. I saw you brush your fingers over these lips, then trace their way down your body."

He does the same with his own fingers while he speaks and Lily blushes.

"How do you feel?"

"A little sore, like you said I might, but mostly I feel alive and happy," she smiles.

"Good," he replies, tightening his grip and pulling her in closer until their faces are mere inches apart.

"What about you? Was I…?"

"Last night was perfect, just like you," he replies before she can finish asking. He leans in for a kiss. His lips brush against hers as he says, "I still don't deserve you, but I have no desire to be without you."

Lily pauses, fighting the desire to have Jack's mouth on hers again. She leans her head back ever so slightly so she can look him in the eyes. "Stop saying you don't deserve me, Jack. You are not your father and I meant every word last night, I want to be with you, whatever that entails, corsair Captaincy included."

Jack nods, a soft smile spreading across his face. "I apologize. When you've lived life a certain way, it's difficult to believe that when someone good comes along, you're worthy of them. But, I feel you in my heart and soul Lily Mearas. Your essence has made a home there and I never want to know what it feels like to not have you part of my life ever again. You've changed me in ways I never thought possible, and you make me want something I hadn't considered for myself since I was young."

"What's that?" she asks softly.

"A family." Jack grazes his thumb across Lily's swollen lower lip. "You're my family now, Lily Mearas. My heart."

Lily gently kisses the pad of his thumb. "And you're mine, Jack Teague."

CHAPTER 8
RECKONING ON THE HORIZON

Lily and Jack round the corner of Eudora's hut hand-in-hand, their skin and hair still slightly damp from jumping off the waterfall as the way to get down from the cliff this morning.

Eudora sits on the porch while the crew eat small bowls of porridge on the steps. They all break out in shit-eating grins when they catch sight of Jack and Lily, but one look from their Captain that clearly conveys *"Don't you dare say a fuckin' word,"* keeps them silent.

Eudora smiles knowingly. "Hot porridge is on the fire. I'll get you some." She rises from her seat, making her way to the hut's entrance.

Lily releases Jack's hand. "I'll help you." She tucks a small section of her loose hair behind her ear then follows Eudora inside.

Eudora scoops the porridge into the two bowls Lily holds. "There's something you want to ask me," she announces.

Lily sighs. "Um, I was wondering, hoping really. Do you have anything that can heal my scars?"

"Mm, can you show me?"

Lily places the bowls on the table then works to unlace the dress. Eudora examines her back carefully, her fingers gently tracing the lines of many of the scars.

"You are strong," she observes in a kind and matter of fact tone. "There are grown men who would not have lasted as long as you did in the time it took to create these."

Lily closes her eyes as a shiver runs down her entire body. "I wish I could take all the credit, that sheer determination to not let Shryke and Staunton win is what drove me to stay alive on the nights when the bleeding was slow to stop and the pain had me curled up on the floor like a wounded dog. But they wanted me to last and ensured I got the right amount of medical attention to achieve that."

Eudora nods. "I see. Unfortunately, there is nothing I can give you for the ones that have completely scarred over as the skin is technically healed, but I do have a salve you can apply for what's still in the process of healing to lighten their appearance."

She spins Lily slightly so she can look her in the eyes. "However, nothing will make either the old or new scars disappear fully."

"I understand."

Lily turns back around as Eudora helps lace up the back of her dress again.

Lily exits the hut, a bowl in each hand, and heads for

Jack. He accepts it, then looks to Eudora. "I, we, can't thank you enough for what you've done."

Eudora waves her hand at him. "Nothing I did tips the balance. How you proceed with the information you now have is up to you."

The crew collects their replenished potion vials then departs Eudora's. Luckily it's all downhill from here so they should make it back to the beach before midday.

Once aboard, Jack scans the deck for Tate. "Set us a course for Mearas Island," he instructs when he finds his navigator.

Tate nods before departing to fetch his map.

Lily steps up beside Jack. "Are you sure you're ready for us to head there?" she asks in a low voice so as not to give the perception that she's challenging him in front of his crew.

Jack takes her hand in his. "No, but we have to, your parents may hold some of the answers you seek. Besides, someone there watched you get taken, and I'd like to have a word with whoever that is."

His dark eyes may be reflecting the bright sunlight, but they're set and serious. As much as Lily wants answers about that mystery man, there's a part of her that already feels sorry for him whenever Jack finds him.

Jack turns to Knox. "I leave it to you to prepare to hoist anchor," he instructs before putting his hand on the small of Lily's back and guiding her to his quarters.

As Knox belays orders, Vane moves to stand beside Turner. He noticed Jack's hand placement on Lily, as well as the look on Turner's face as they walked away.

"What happened on Molai?" he asks gruffly. "Yesterday she would barely look at him and today she's letting him touch her."

Turner keeps his eyes forward and his voice low. "I don't know, but I'm pretty sure they fucked. She went off into the jungle last night after whatever Eudora did to get her memories back, Captain followed not too much later. They didn't come back until early this morning, and when they did, everything was different."

"What do you mean, 'different'?"

"They were holding hands, and when the guys almost started to cheer, the look Captain gave shut 'em up real quick. I wager it was because she's a high-born lady and he didn't want us to embarrass her, but..."

Vane crosses his arms over his chest. "Damn it," he hisses. "No, it's not that. I knew there was something about her. He's been different since she woke up. He's had women before, but he never let any of them get close. This one's close."

Turner shrugs. "Maybe, but they both know it'll never work between them. They're from completely opposite worlds, and while her father may be grateful for her return, no governor would let his precious daughter fall in love with a pirate, especially the Captain of the Savage Sea. This'll be over when we reach Mearas Island."

Vane grunts. "We'll see."

~

126

The Savage Sea rocks gently from side to side as it glides over the waves. Jack sits on the edge of his bed gazing down at Lily, who's sleeping soundly on her stomach, the upper part of her back uncovered, leaving her scars exposed.

Jack passes his fingertips over them softly, feeling every bump and divot. He smiles ever so slightly as the memories of him kissing them earlier that night come back to him. It was the second time they'd slept together since Molai and he couldn't get enough of her. He'd spend all day, every day in bed with Lily if he could, but with less than a week to go until they reach Mearas, he really needed to focus on a plan for not only getting her safely to her parents, but also speaking with the governor without getting himself or his crew arrested.

As much as he believed in Lily, he'd never met her father, and based on experience, he knew a politician couldn't be trusted, especially with the news he and Lily had to share. In his heart, Jack recognizes it won't be as simple as telling her father she's choosing a life outside what he and her mother had planned; there would be trouble.

Lily had said she wanted to be with him, that she wanted adventure and freedom in her life, but not only was piracy itself dangerous, anyone living the corsair life was at inherent risk, including the women; especially his woman. The wife of a corsair Captain, particularly the Captain of the Savage Sea? All it would take is for the wrong person to find Lily and they'd have Jack on his knees. In fact, he was beginning to feel that he'd rather give up this life and settle on land with her than expose her to the true dangers of it.

The men with families kept them on Havara Island for safety, but despite the protections they'd put in place, he was unsure if it would be safe enough for her.

Lily stirs at Jack's touch and turns her head to face him.

"I didn't mean to wake you," he says softly.

"It's okay. What are you doing awake?"

"Just thinking."

Lily rolls onto her side as Jack's hand slowly falls from her back. She pulls the sheet up to cover her more from the slight chill in the cabin, then takes his hand in hers. "Tell me," she prods. "Don't treat me like I can't handle whatever's bothering you. Share your thoughts and burdens with me."

Jack admits his concerns about Mearas and what her parents, particularly her father, will do when they divulge their intentions.

"I love you, and we will be together, but I need to protect this crew. As Captain, they're my responsibility, and a number of them have families," he concludes.

"And yourself," she adds. "Without you there's no us."

"Very true."

"Come here." She gently pulls at his arm while she slides over on the bed.

Jack lowers himself next to her.

Lily places her free hand along the side of his face. "We won't rush to tell them about us. Let's focus on Shryke, have my father take care of him, Staunton and their entire operation first, then, when that's all settled, we'll approach them about my decision. I know it won't be easy, and since the safety of you and this crew is paramount, if I have to tell them through a letter, I will."

Jack sighs. "After everything you and they have been through these past three years, you can't do that."

"I can, and I will if it's the only way to do so without endangering your life."

"I love you," he confesses while pulling her close, giving her a deep kiss.

Lily wraps her arms around his shoulder as she works to shimmy beneath him.

He breaks away when he realizes what she's done, giving their bodies a once over. "Something I can do for you, *little flower*?" he teases.

She smiles wryly up at him, her eyes heated with desire. "You know there is, *Captain*."

~

The next day, Jack strategizes with Knox and Turner about getting Lily from the ship to the governor's villa, while she approaches Vane on the main deck.

Vane watches out of the corner of his eye, continuing to go about his business of sharpening his blade. He's surprised to see her wearing a pair of black britches with what's likely one of Jack's white shirts tucked into them, instead of a dress.

"Vane?" she asks once she's standing in front of him.

He grunts in response, not stopping what he's doing.

"Captain Teague told me you're the weapons and training master on the crew. I was wondering, would you teach me some basic ways to defend myself before we reach Mearas?"

Vane pauses and looks up at her. "Pardon?"

"I'd like to learn how to defend myself, no matter how basic. Anything's better than what I know now, which is nothing."

He narrows his eyes at her. "Isn't that beneath a woman of your standing? Don't delicate creatures such as yourself rely on the protection of others your whole lives?"

Lily crosses her arms. She knew Vane didn't like her, but this is approaching ridiculous. The rest of the crew seems to have accepted who she is to Jack, but Vane is still as gruff and mean as when they first met.

"That's how my life has been, yes, but once my father deals with Shryke I'll be giving up that life for one with Jack, and I know that comes with risks. He won't always be around, and I refuse to be helpless."

Vane stands abruptly. "What did you say?"

Lily uncrosses her arms, letting them fall to her sides. "Jack and I, well, I won't be staying on Mearas after Shryke's dealt with. Once it's safe to leave Mearas I'll be going to Havara, where Knox's wife, Ellie, along with the other women and families of the crew reside. I know it's protected to a degree, but I'd be more comfortable if I knew I stood a fighting chance should something happen. Please, teach me."

Vane's head spins with this information. He knew she

was going to fuck things up for this crew. Jack's a great Captain, but he knows that if Jack has a woman he cares about somewhere, there's a chance he'll eventually want to give up the Captaincy; a true loss to their crew and the ship's reputation.

He thinks for a moment. Maybe if he can show Jack that Lily doesn't have what it takes to be his woman, Jack will change his mind. He takes a deep breath, then says, "All right, grab a sword."

Lily looks hesitantly at the few lying around him. "We're not going to start with something a little lighter? Or made of wood?"

"Look, we're only a few days from Mearas. If you're serious about my help, you'll start with what I tell you, because once we're there, this ends."

Lily nods slowly then moves to pick up one of the thinner foils while Vane gets himself into position. The foil's slightly heavier than she expected but she's able to hold it properly, albeit with some concentrated effort. *"Guess these last three years hauling heavy buckets of water around Agrego were good for something,"* she thinks sarcastically.

Vane begins reviewing how best to stand and hold the sword. He can tell she's struggling, but registers the determination on her face. He very slowly starts swinging his sword at her while verbally instructing her how to clash hers with his defensively.

Jack watches from the bridge, impressed by Lily's determination and grateful to his sword master for taking the time to teach her. After a few minutes, he goes back to his meeting with Knox and Turner.

"I do think the best option for first arrival is for me, Knox and George to get Lily to the governor's villa," he announces as he steps back up to the group. "The less intimidating we look, the better, otherwise I'd have you come along, Turner."

"Understood," Turner replies.

Knox turns to him. "In my absence, I leave it to you to get the cargo unloaded and to the merchants for selling, and have the crew start replenishing supplies."

Turner nods.

~

A few hours later, members of the crew have gathered on deck, watching Lily and Vane continue their training. It's clear she's tired, but she's refusing to yield.

"Be careful," Vane says halfheartedly. "Exhaustion can and often does cost you."

"How so?" Lily asks. It's a genuine question. She's tired, but she still feels like she has strength left to continue.

"You want me to show you?"

"Yes."

"All right. You asked for it."

Vane speeds up his movements, and it becomes clear to Lily very quickly that she can no longer keep up.

A gust of wind billows down the back of her shirt and Vane seizes his opportunity. He swings in a way that forces Lily to compromise her stance and turn at a slight angle. This allows him to slice up the back of the shirt as Lily drops to one knee. He rests the tip of his sword at the base of her neck while she attempts to catch her breath.

"See?" he asks sardonically.

Suddenly, a blade is inserted below his. The holder quickly sweeps his up and away from Lily's neck.

"What the fuck are you doing?!" Jack bellows while using his strength to disarm Vane, the tip of his sword coming to rest just below Vane's chin.

Jack's eyes are alight with anger. "Answer me!" he demands.

Vane holds his stance as a hush falls over the crew. "She," he begins.

"She?" Jack asks before Vane can continue. "Her name's Lily. *Lily* is my woman, and you *will* treat her and her name with the same respect you treat me," he hisses.

"Jack," Lily begins, still in her half kneel. "It's not Vane's fault, he warned me about not knowing when to yield and I underestimated my level of tiredness."

Jack keeps his eyes locked on Vane, nostrils still flared. "He knows better."

"Jack," Lily calls out again.

This time, Jack lowers his sword and turns to face her. It's then that he realizes why the crew has fallen so silent. The slash Vane created along the back of her shirt was long enough to cause it to fall open in a way that exposes a good portion of her scarred back.

Lily hasn't moved yet because she's holding the front of the shirt in place to prevent it from completely falling off her shoulders.

Jack's eyes widen as he looks from her back to the men's faces. He quickly sheethes his sword, grabs the fabric loosely hanging from Lily's shoulders to hold it in place, then helps her stand.

Lily looks around the deck, taking in the faces staring back at her. They're full of pity, some shock and definitely discomfort. She holds her head high, adjusts her shoulders and hold on the fabric, then turns to Vane. "Thank you for the lesson," she says with sincere appreciation.

The crew slowly parts as she passes between them, making her way to Jack's cabin.

Jack looks to Vane with a steely gaze, but says no more before following after Lily.

Knox picks up Lily's foil where it fell. "Be prepared," he says in an even tone to the sword master. "I can promise you, her word will decide your fate." He passes Vane the foil before turning to the crew. "Show's over, everyone back to work."

The crew silently disperses while Vane stands in his spot, replaying not only what he's done, but also the sight of the numerous scars on Lily's back. He had no idea.

Once inside Jack's quarters, Lily rips the rest of the shirt and lets it fall down her arms. Jack walks through the door as the discarded fabric settles on the floor.

"Are you all right?" he asks, as he moves to stand in front of her.

Lily's eyes are slightly misty but she nods. "Now they understand why you did what you did when Staunton boarded. That makes it worth it," she replies, shoulders slightly dipped.

Jack shakes his head slowly. "No, they never needed to see this to understand. I'm their Captain, the orders I give, and the decisions I make don't require justification unless I feel like providing those details. You say the word and Vane will suffer consequences for what he did."

Lily steps up to him, resting the palms of her hands on his chest. "Like I said on deck, I asked him to push me. I was being stubborn. He did what I asked, that's all. I don't want you to do anything."

"But."

"No buts, Jack. It's my body. You asked, and I'm telling you not to retaliate. You need Vane and you know it. I won't be an excuse or reason for your crew to lose such a valuable member, okay?"

Jack huffs slightly but nods his agreement. "Okay. Now, let's find you something else to wear because if your bare breasts stay exposed to me any longer I'm not going to be able to control myself."

Lily backs away slowly, a playful smile spreading across her face. "Would losing control be a bad thing? Surely the Captain can spare a few minutes."

Jack's eyes heat with desire. "Oh, little flower, if I'm going to have you it'll be longer than a few measly minutes, and I really should continue my planning with Knox and Turner."

Lily loosens the belt holding the oversized britches up, loops her fingers inside the band, then shimmies her hips a little to allow them to fall to the floor. "Understood, my Captain. I'll just slip into some new clothes then join you on deck."

She watches as his eyes become slightly hooded, his hands moving to the knot around his waist holding his sword and dagger in place. The sound of the items hitting the wood floor echoes slightly.

"Fuck it," he declares in a soft, but husky voice while closing the gap between them.

Jack wraps his arms around Lily's waist and lifts. She encircles his hips with her legs as he presses her back into the wall. His grip tightens around her thighs, the electric passion between them growing.

Jack's lips slowly graze along Lily's jaw as she lets out a breathy gasp.

"Please," she begs, her voice barely above a whisper.

Jack nips at her lower lip before spinning around and carrying her to his desk. He quickly sweeps the maps onto the floor with one hand before lowering her on it.

CHAPTER 9
THE PRICE OF POWER

Lily, Jack, Knox and George make their way through the port of Mearas Island with trepidation. Despite the heat, Lily wears a hooded cloak to conceal her face, trusting the man she loves, and his crew, to not only be her eyes, but protectors as well.

Her father may be the governor, but they've all agreed there's a distinct possibility some of Shryke's men may be here, despite not seeing the Intrepid in the harbor on arrival, and they could intercept them before reaching the villa if they're not careful.

She's so close to being home, Lily dreads to think what could happen should the wrong person recognize her.

Dusk approaches, and for their own safety, Lily wants the men back on the ship, ready to set sail should the need arise.

As they stand at the foot of the carriage drive below the villa, Lily hugs the tender-hearted Knox goodbye.

"It's been a pleasure," he offers.

Lily nods. She then smiles at George. "Thank you both," she replies. "I'd literally be lost without you."

"Keep an eye on the street," Jack instructs them.

He finds it somewhat strange there are no guards, but Lily assures him it's nothing to worry about, and common for them to not be present at this hour. "They'll be here after nightfall," she'd said as they approached the drive.

Knox and George stand at attention but with a slight casual posture so as not to attract prying eyes. The street in front of the villa isn't heavily trafficked but it's best to still be prepared.

As Lily and Jack walk up the hill she can feel her heart quicken, unsure of what's about to happen. During their ascent up the front steps, she grabs Jack's hand for comfort. It doesn't stop him from walking, but he holds hers tightly as well.

They pause in front of the door, glance at one another, then Jack reaches for the door knocker. He raps it against its base three times then looks down at Lily. The uncertainty of their future together, and the very real prospect of having to break his promise and let her go weighs heavily on him.

A middle-age man in a powdered wig and navy blue dress coat answers the door. He looks down at them with a skeptical expression. "Yes?"

Lily withdraws her hand from Jack's and lowers the hood of her cloak.

The man's jaw drops as the color drains from his face. "Miss. Lily? Oh heaven's me... please, come inside."

She smiles softly. "Hello, Darcy."

After Lily and Jack step through the door into the foyer, Darcy scans around outside before shutting it behind him. He pivots to face the pair, looking Lily up and down.

"Where are my mother and father?" she asks without hesitation.

Darcy briefly glances at Jack, unease settling within him. "Let me get the governor. W-w-wait here." His hands tremble as he hurries away and up the grand staircase.

Lily turns in a slow circle, trying to take everything in. It's been three years, but the house is exactly as she remembers it.

Jack scans what he can see. The villa looks exactly how he figured it would, ornate decor, the most expensive furniture in tones that reflect the tropical locale. His eyes sweep to the sitting room off the foyer, where a large family portrait hangs above a fireplace. He's taken by how much Lily really does look like her mother.

"How are you doing?" Jack prompts, tearing his eyes from the image.

Lily takes a deep inhale. "Slightly overwhelmed. Nervous. It's all so familiar to me but also feels like a different lifetime."

Jack's inclined to ask her why she's found cause to be nervous, but a commotion from above stops him. Their attention is drawn to the balcony overhead as a frantic-looking man appears. He's pale, and shows signs of balding.

"Lily?" he whispers, leaning over the balcony.

Lily stares up at him, tears brimming in her eyes. Jack presumes this is her father and watches as the man withdraws from their sight until he begins descending the stairs.

Lily runs right into his arms as they're both overcome with emotion.

"Oh, my girl, my dear, sweet child." Governor Mearas holds his daughter tightly against him, heart pounding. He glances at Jack a few times, then holds Lily at arms length to look at her. "Where have you been?"

Lily backs away from her father, takes Jack by the arm, then guides him to stand in front of her father. He looks from his daughter to Jack and back again.

"Your daughter's been a prisoner of Commander Shryke on Agrego these past three years. She recently escaped, and my crew and I were able to aid her." Jack leaves out what happened on the Dawning, a choice he and Lily agreed to prior to disembarking. The less her father knew about that, the better.

Governor Mearas cradles his daughter's head in his hands, confusion and disbelief etched across his face. "Agrego? You mean you've only been a weeks' sail away this entire time?"

Lily nods slowly.

"Did you not think to search there while looking for her?" Jack prods.

Governor Mearas's gaze snaps to Jack as he releases Lily's face. "And just who the hell are you to question me in that way? Why would I ever think that Commander Shryke took my daughter? We thought it was some criminals, some pirates." His face has reddened as anger and something Jack can't quite place rises within him.

Jack scoffs. "Shryke is a criminal, he's just one that benefits the island governors, who in turn benefit the emperor, so you all allow it."

The governor takes a defensive stance between his daughter and the man who still hasn't answered his question about who he is. "Listen here, I'm grateful for the return of my daughter, but don't forget who you're speaking to."

Lily steps between them as she realizes the situation's devolving faster than she thought it would. "Father, please, it's only the three of us here and Captain Teague is simply stating what we all already know."

"Teague? You've brought a pirate into my home?"

The surprise on his face, followed by immediate revulsion isn't lost on Lily. She needs to get them to the point before the night guards arrive and she completely loses control of a situation she's barely holding onto.

"Father, I would be dead without this man and his crew. Listen to me."

She takes her father's hands, holding them tightly, then recounts what's happened to her since that day on the beach. She leaves out certain details, including the full truth about the Dawning. She divulges Thompson's ultimate plans for her, and that Jack rescued her from that fate.

Her father interrupts to ask what she means about her stolen memories.

"We found someone who was able to help restore Lily's memories of the time between her kidnapping and

Agrego. It was a painful process for her, but your daughter's strong, and determined. The problem is, the retrieved memories don't provide answers as to why she was taken in the first place," Jack interjects.

"What? How is that possible?" The governor can barely believe what he's hearing.

Lily looks to her father. "The clearing of the magic that did this only restored things I saw and heard. Nothing that was said or done told me why. Do you know why Shryke would want me? All he ever said was that it was mother's fault, but he never gave any details."

The governor's eyes grow a little wary.

"You have to understand, Governor Mearas, when Lily was brought aboard my ship, all I knew was that when I looked at your daughter I couldn't fathom how such a young woman would be sentenced to a place like Agrego. Now that we know the truth from Shryke's perspective, any information you or Lady Mearas can provide would be most helpful."

Lily nods at her father in agreement, eyes wide and pleading. "He's telling the truth." Lily looks around, then back at her father. She hasn't heard any other noise within the villa and had expected her mother to be here already, but perhaps she's out. "Speaking of, where is mother?"

The governor lets out a sigh as he steps back, his expression sad. He turns away from them slowly. "I am so sorry my child," he whispers gently. "But she is gone."

Lily's heart sinks. What does he mean by 'gone?' She moves to stand directly in front of her father, but he can hardly look at her.

"She died about a year after you were taken. The doctor said it was from a broken heart."

"No," she gasps, sinking down onto the stairs.

The governor kneels in front of his daughter while Jack fights the urge to comfort Lily. He knows he has to keep his distance while in the governor's presence.

"I don't understand," Lily declares softly. "She died because of me?"

"No," Jack and her father respond at the same time.

Governor Mearas shoots Jack a look of displeasure at the fact that a pirate dared insert himself in this conversation. He lifts Lily's chin with his fingers. "It's not your fault," he says softly. "What happened was a terrible tragedy, that's all."

~

Lily stands with Jack by the front door. Despite his protest, the pouch of gold coins her father insisted he take for returning her are tucked into his belt. She doesn't want him to go, but she needs Jack and his crew safe while her father takes a stand against Shryke.

After much careful discussion, Governor Mearas agreed to consult with the other governors to deal with Shryke. He would not divulge much information to his daughter, nor to the pirate she seemed to trust. The truth was that he needed to be careful how Shryke was handled given his power and influence.

Chalking his daughters trust in Jack up to the fact that she'd been sheltered, was desperate for assistance when she escaped Agrego, and didn't know much about the world - she was a woman after all - until he knew more, he'd have to at least provide the illusion that he was willing to take anything the pirate said seriously.

Lily leans against Jack's shoulder knowing her father isn't anywhere in sight. "When will we see each other again?"

"I will come to see you as often as I can until this is all settled," Jack replies softly.

Lily smirks. "A pirate sneaking into the governor's villa? Scandalous!"

A grin materializes from the corner of Jack's mouth and she can't help but think about kissing him again.

"Yes, I'm not too sure your father would approve, but nothing can keep me away from you." Jack takes Lily's hands firmly in his. "Promise you'll get word to me as soon as your father has a plan. We'll likely depart Mearas for one of the neighboring islands in a few days, but will return once we offload as much of our cargo as possible."

"I wll." She doesn't want him to go and tries to memorize every inch of him at this moment.

The light is quickly fading from the room as the sun continues to set.

"I must go," he adds. The thought of leaving her was tearing him up inside, but her safety was of the utmost importance, and the safest place for her right now was hidden at home. So, he lifts her hands until they're just below his lips, then places a kiss on the top of them.

"I'll see you soon, little flower."

She stands in the doorway watching as he makes his descent down the drive, never looking back.

"I love you," she thinks.

When Jack reaches Knox and George the three men turn right, disappearing behind the tall trees, ultimately blocking them from Lily's view. She slowly shuts the door, then turns back into the foyer, leaning against it.

~

A little more than a week has passed since Lily's return home. She'd come to an agreement with her father that they would not risk making a big deal of her return for fear of Shryke finding out, so she'd been spending all of her time within the confines of the villa.

Instead of conducting business from the residence, Governor Mearas began taking meetings in town so Lily could have use of the house, but even then, the limited staff he kept on were sworn to absolute secrecy.

Sitting in the shade on her balcony facing the sea, Lily's thoughts drift to Jack and she wonders where the wind has carried him and his crew.

He'd said he would come to see her, but her father had informed her that the Savage Sea sailed from the bay two days ago. She mindlessly twirls a piece of her hair, a sadness settling in her chest at Jack departing without sending word.

This place she's been returned to doesn't feel much

like home anymore. In fact, in the days since she's been back, she's felt more alone than she thought she would. With her mother gone, father now in town for most of every day, and a limited staff who barely bothered speaking more than a few words to her at her father's behest, she found herself wishing more and more that she was still aboard the Savage Sea with Jack.

She can feel the warm sun mixed with the gentle breeze lulling her to sleep and she settles into it. It's a reprieve she's grateful for given that she also hasn't been feeling well since her return.

"Likely all of the stress," her father remarked when Lily could barely stomach some porridge at breakfast that morning.

~

Lily's awoken by the sound of her father calling up to her from the foyer. She rises and walks through her bedroom to the interior of the house. Once there, she looks over the railing at her father, who stands at the foot of the stairs.

"Come Lily, we have much to discuss."

"Finally," she thinks, believing it to be an update on dealing with Shryke.

Governor Mearas holds out his hand as he waits for Lily to descend the stairs. It's taking everything in him to remain calm and not present any cause for her to worry.

Once Lily arrives at the foot of the stairs she takes his hand, allowing him to lead her toward their dining room. She looks at the marble floor, not wanting her father to see the mix of emotions she's feeling about everything that's transpired, how she now feels about home, and her love for Jack.

Her father had also been somewhat distant since her return. Lily figured it had to do with the shock of it all, but she'd expected a little more relief and compassion from him. She hadn't shown her father the scars nor told him every detail of the last three years, but had provided some insight into what she'd been through. Even then, it felt like he was keeping his distance to some degree.

When they enter the dining room she lifts her head, expecting to see the table set for an early super. Instead, what she sees drains the blood from her body as her stomach drops.

"Hello, Lily." Staunton leans against the table, arms crossed casually in front of his chest. "You're quite the elusive escapee, my dear."

Lily freezes. She quickly looks from him to her father, who she realizes can't meet her eyes. Lily withdraws her hand from his with little effort, then takes a step backward.

"Tsk, tsk, tsk," Staunton warns, his eyes narrowing at her.

As if his warning was some sort of command, soldiers materialize, coming in from the servant's door to the kitchen and the one she just entered through, effectively cutting Lily off from escaping the room.

Fear now envelopes her and it suddenly feels hard to breathe.

Staunton pushes himself away from the table, striding to stand in front of her. "I must say, the sun has done you wonders. You look more radiant than ever." He takes a strand of her hair and twirls it around his fingers before gently bringing it up to his nostrils and inhaling her scent.

Lily swings her head to the right; she can't bear to look at him, or her father. How could he of all people betray her after everything she'd told him?

"Thank you, Governor Mearas." Staunton doesn't take his eyes off Lily while he speaks. "You have been most helpful in returning my future bride."

He smirks, waiting for her reaction.

Lily snaps her head back to look at Staunton. "What did you just say?"

He smiles wryly at her, but the look on his face is terrifying. "Yes," he hisses. "Commander Shryke and I agreed that it's time for me to take a wife to elevate my position and increase his power and influence. Who better than the daughter of Mearas Island's governor? After all, once this little adventure is all settled, I'll be hailed a hero for orchestrating your return."

Staunton finally turns to look at her father. "As promised, Commander Shryke will ensure your stay here in the governor's villa continues."

Lily glares at her father. "Father, what is he talking about?"

Governor Mearas finally looks at her, shame and defeat etched on his face.

"What have you done?" Her voice cracks.

Before he can say anything, Staunton draws his saber and plunges it into the governor's lower chest. Lily startles backward with a scream, right into the arms of one of the soldiers.

Her father makes a hollow wheezing sound as Staunton pulls the saber from his body. He sinks down against the wall until he's seated on the floor, his blood quickly staining the white marble as it quickly oozes through the open wound.

Governor Mearas looks down at his chest, then up at Staunton in bewilderment. "Why?" he mouths.

Staunton crouches in front of him, using the governor's pants to clean the blood off his saber. "Because, power comes to those who dare to take it, not those who snivel and grovel for any little bit of what they can get. With you gone, the Commander's power will continue to grow, especially once we deem it suitable for Lily and I to return and assume the governorship."

Staunton leans in closer and speaks in a low, malevolent tone only the governor can hear. "Die with the knowledge that Commander Shryke has now taken everything from you, you piss poor excuse of a man."

Lily struggles against the grip of the soldier, but her efforts are futile. Her father slowly bobs his head to the side to look at her, his breathing becoming increasingly shallow as his eyes start to gloss over.

"And you," Staunton continues, as he stands, looking down at Lily with taunting eyes. "The Commander and I are terribly upset with you."

Lily spits at him, which lands just below Staunton's left eye. "You're both monsters," she hisses.

Without flinching, he wipes it away with his sleeve. "Well, I guess that answers my question about you coming willingly. Such a pity. But, don't worry my dear, I'll have you behaving like the proper lady you were born to be in no time."

"I will never marry you," she shoots back as she strains against the grip of the soldier holding her.

He chuckles. "Oh Lily, it's sweet you think you have a choice." Staunton leans in close to her right ear. "I'm so looking forward to our wedding night."

Lily snaps at him with her teeth, but misses and Staunton grimaces. "I see your time with the pirates has only worsened your attitude. I'll remedy that."

With the snap of his fingers, another soldier appears, tipping a glass vial into a handkerchief. The man hands it to Staunton and Lily stiffens as the one holding her tightens his grip.

"If only you'd learn to behave. Looks like I'll have my work cut out for me once we're wed," Staunton remarks in a threatening tone before pressing the handkerchief over her nose and mouth.

At first she struggles, but within a few seconds the room around Lily begins to blur before fading to black. The last thing she does is scream for Jack in her mind. Her body goes limp and the soldier who'd been holding her in place catches her as she falls.

"All right, let's go," Staunton commands. "I want to set sail quickly and quietly. That damn pirate is still around and the last thing we need is him catching wind of this."

Teague had lied to him once, and based on his conversation with Governor Mearas earlier about Lily's return, he assumes it's because of the reward. As much as he'd like to dispose of the scum himself, that will have to wait until he returns with the full power of a governorship and Shryke behind him. Until then, Staunton will let the entire crew live on borrowed time.

"Yes Captain," the men respond.

The soldier cradles Lily in his arms then follows the others out the back door, past the bodies of the house staff.

Staunton sneers down at the dying governor. "Pleasure doing business with you, Governor. Rest assured that your daughter is in very capable hands. "Darcy!" he calls.

The house manager shuffles into the room, head bowed.

Staunton turns to him. "Remember our deal?"

Darcy nods rapidly.

"Go to the governor's office and tell the staff that due to family matters, he requests to be left alone for a few days. Then, return to your sister's apartment."

"Wh-what about the bodies?"

Staunton sniffles as he looks from the governor's almost lifeless body to the ones he can see in the kitchen. "Let them rot here until they're discovered by someone else."

Darcy nods again then follows Staunton out the back door as Governor Mearas draws his final breaths, all strength gone from his body.

~

Two days later, Jack stands at the edge of the dock while the remainder of the supplies are loaded onto the longboats bound for the Savage Sea anchored out in the harbor.

They've been on Mearas longer than he intended, but there was a delay in getting some of the items they needed to resupply the ship. And, if he was being completely honest with himself, he thinks, as he stares up at the governor's villa on the hill, part of him was hoping to see Lily one last time before they set sail.

He hadn't heard from her since parting the night she returned home, but he'd gotten two letters to Darcy to deliver to her. Given her father's power, he figured she was just being cautious by not responding. He still felt that bringing her back was the right decision, but he couldn't shake the gnawing feeling that she'd need him sooner rather than later.

Night had fallen on Mearas, and after spending more time in the tavern than he should have, he wanted to set sail before he changed his mind about leaving Lily, even for the short time it would take to sell their new goods.

"Captain! Captain!"

Jack looks up the dock to see George running full speed down toward him and Knox.

"George, what is it?" Knox asks once he's reached them.

The lad struggles to speak and catch his breath at the same time.

"Easy, deep breaths," Knox coaches.

George would have complied with Knox's instructions, but there wasn't time and he had so much to share. "In the tavern... soldiers... weeks."

Jack and Knox look at George, confusion etched on their faces.

"What does that have to do with us?" Jack inquires. "Soldiers come and go from the taverns all the time without bothering the crew. The government of this island has never given us trouble, and I highly doubt they will now that Lily has been returned safely. Help finish loading the ship so we can be underway." He turns to walk away.

George sucks in as much air as he can. "Staunton!" he shouts, but not so loudly as to draw attention from others outside their crew.

Jack freezes then spins on his heels. "What about him?"

"This woman at the tavern was getting flirty with me. She mentioned his name, and that she was glad he and his men were gone. I gave her a few coins to give me more details. She said he was pretty rough with one of their best girls while he was here, a young redhead. She pointed the girl out to me as she spoke. Captain, this girl looks so similar to Lily."

"I'm sorry to hear that, truly, but she said she was glad he was gone." Jack motions to the harbor. "The Intrepid's not here, so they must've set sail before we arrived."

George shakes his head vigorously. "No, Captain, she said she last saw him three days ago."

Knox quickly turns his gaze to Jack, but Jack's eyes are already honed in on the direction of the villa. Without hesitation, he dashes down the ramp, sprinting right past his quartermaster. Knox calls after him but Jack doesn't turn back, his energy focused on reaching the villa as fast as possible.

Jack skids to a stop in the foyer, sword in one hand, cocked pistol in the other.

The home was dark and no one had answered the door when he pounded on it, but it'd been unlocked so it opened with ease.

There's an odor in the home, one he was all too familiar with; death.

His heart thunders at the thought of something having happened to Lily, especially when he was still so close. Jack approaches the dining room slowly, listening intensely for any signs of life.

The sound of boots hitting the pebbles outside gives him pause though and he swivels back toward the front door, just in time to see George stumble through it. Jack quickly puts his finger to his lips as George straightens, slowly drawing his own sword and dagger. Jack motions to the dining room and the two of them creep down the short hallway.

With both men pressed against the wall, Jack counts to three with his fingers, then spins into a wide stance in the middle of the open doorway, George quick to follow beside him.

Even in the dim light, Jack's eyes are immediately

drawn to the blood-stained marble floor, Governor Mearas's lifeless body positioned haphazardly, having collapsed there as he drew his final breath, all color now drained from his limbs.

"No, no, no!" Jack exclaims, hastily kneeling down next to the governor, feeling the coldness of his skin.

"Staunton," Jack whispers, rage rising inside him like a fire. He knows there's no need to search the rest of the house, Lily isn't here.

Jack stands then begins making his way back to the front door with George right behind him.

"What are we going to do Captain?" George pulls the door shut as they exit the villa.

There's zero hesitation in Jack's response, his steely gaze focused on the horizon, knowing Staunton has at least a two-day head start. "Find Lily, then kill Shryke and Staunton."

CHAPTER 10
STAUNTON'S FINAL CONQUEST

Captain Antony Staunton pushes open the doors to the main hall with immense pride. He'd found Lily, and taken care of the governor, following Shryke's orders implicitly, and it was finally time for his just reward.

He's so consumed with the thought of it that he ignores the sounds of Lily struggling in her manacles as her captors lead her down the hall behind him.

Shryke looks up from his meal, a sick smile spreading across his face.

Lily's wide, fearful eyes lock onto his.

"Well, well, look who we have here!" He wipes his hands and mouth with a cloth as he rises, then saunters to where Staunton has come to a stop. Shryke looks hard at Lily, who has stopped struggling, then at Staunton, before clapping his hand on Staunton's shoulder. "Well done, Captain. I knew I could count on you."

"Thank you, Sir," Staunton replies, bowing his head and stepping to the side so Shryke can pass.

With Shryke's face inches from her own, Lily shudders. His breath is stale and horrid.

"You led us on quite the chase," he muses.

Lily glares at him. "You killed my parents. Why?"

A cheshire grin slips up his face, but he doesn't reply.

"Answer me you fucking monster!" she demands.

Shryke chuckles. "Such a word dares to come from your noble lips? I hope you're ready Captain, she's going to be a handful to retrain."

The two men stand shoulder to shoulder, looking down at Lily, judgement and delight in their eyes, as the soldiers on either side of her force her to her knees.

"Don't worry Commander, I assure you she's nothing I can't handle."

Lily gulps, her throat parched, stomach in absolute knots as reality slams into her. She now sees no end to the nightmare that is these two men.

She releases a long exhale as her shoulders slump. No one is coming for her; the only person who knows she's here is her dead father, so whenever Jack sails back to Mearas, no one there will have any idea what to tell him.

"He'll figure it out though, he has to," she thinks to herself. The question is, if what Staunton said on Mearas is true, he'll have an entire navy at his disposal. What could Jack and his crew reasonably do against such power?

"Commander Shryke, please. Please, just tell me why you've done all of this. I still don't understand what my mother did to you."

Shryke cocks his head at her change of tone, then crouches down in front of Lily, slipping his fingers below her chin, forcing her to look up at him.

"When I was young, I didn't come from much. I did what I had to do to ensure my family could put some food on the table, and I was hired as a young boy to run errands for your grandfather. During my comings and goings from the estate, I met your mother."

Although still looking at Lily, his eyes glass over as the memories fill his mind. "She was the kindest thing, always sneaking me some extra food, or sweets. Over the years, I fell in love with her, and made a promise that I'd make something of myself so that when we were older I'd be worthy of her love."

"But as the years went by and your grandparents set their expectations for who your mother was to become, she pulled away from me. I saw her less and less, until one day, after I returned from my first tour of duty, she walked right by me on a garden path, head held high. She didn't even acknowledge I was there." His face is a mix of anger and disappointment. "A few weeks later, she was engaged to your father, the son of a governor and who was set to become one himself."

Lily slowly shakes her head as she squints her eyes. "So, you waited over 20 years to kidnap her child as what, some sort of revenge because she didn't feel the same way about you as you did her?" she asks, incredulously.

Shryke stands abruptly. "No! She did feel the same, I know it. She gave in to the expectations set upon her based on her birth. She was too weak to stand up to her parents, tell them she loved me... but look at me now."

He gestures wildly around the room. "I did what I needed to do. I'm a Commander in the Emperor's navy, the most powerful slave trader across all the isles. Governors and the crown line their coffers because of me." He stops and looks back down at Lily. "Including your father, until his greed got too big for his own good and he thought he could exert power over me," he chuckles.

"So, I took action. I knew taking you would destroy your mother's heart, something I'd waited so long to do to make her feel the way she'd made me feel."

Lily was actively holding back her tears. "You're a madman," she hisses.

"Oh no, darling, I'm calculated." He reaches down, takes hold of her manacles and pulls Lily up from the floor. "There's a difference," he smirks in response.

"Tell me one thing. Why did you have that witch make me forget those moments between being taken and the day I woke up in that cell? I was able to get those memories back, but other than you making a comment about my mother while I was strapped to that table, nothing worth forgetting happened, so I really don't understand."

Staunton steps forward, a slight grin on his disgusting face. "Well, Commander, it sounds like we really didn't need the witch at all. If she got her memories back and still doesn't know, then she never saw him in the first place."

Shryke looks appraisingly at Lily, whose confusion is written all over her face. "Yes, it seems so," he muses, then leans in closer to her. "Your father was there that day on the beach, when my men took you."

The world around her blurs as a loud ringing in her

ears and the sound of her own breathing overwhelms Lily. "What?" she croaks out through a throat as dry as a desert, while her head swims and the hall appears to get slightly blurry.

"When you first arrived, I wanted you to be hopeful, to believe that one day your parents would come rescue you. Made it a bit more fun for me, you see." Shryke shimmies his shoulders a little in excitement.

"But, it's true. He was there that day, watching from the treeline, too cowardly to show his face, but clearly couldn't help himself from seeing what he'd agreed to. According to Staunton's report, there was a moment while you were being rendered unconscious where your body sort of spun around as you fell and Staunton here thought you'd caught a glimpse of your father before passing out. So, just in case that was true, I had your memories from that moment until you woke up here wiped, ensuring you'd forget any conversations you may have also overheard on the ship that pertained to your parents in any way."

Lily backs away from him and into the guards behind her, who don't move an inch. She's a ball of nerves, panic, disgust, and heartbreak over this revelation, as the memory of the unknown soldier verbally making an observation to Staunton about a man in the trees replays in her mind.

It's taking everything in her to push down the bile now rising in her throat at the thought of her father making such a monstrous betrayal, all for the sake of his position.

"My father traded me for power?"

Shryke swivels his head from side to side. "Mm, more like made a sacrifice. He overestimated his power, I reminded him just how much of it was due to my own goodwill, et voila, here you are."

"You and my father are vile," Lily states softly but firmly.

Shryke waves his hand at her dismissively. "Yes, yes, we already know how you feel. But, I'm the one who's still alive, unlike your parents."

Her eyes narrow. "One day you will pay for your crimes, I promise you," she fires back through gritted teeth.

Shryke and Staunton chuckle as Shryke claps him lightly on the back. "She's all yours, Captain."

"Thank you, Commander."

Staunton tugs harshly on the chain of Lily's manacles, pulling her into him. He strokes the side of her cheek and she stiffens. His eyes are focused, with a glint of something Lily can't place, and just like in the memory from her first journey here and interaction with him in the cell on the ship, fear continues to rise within her.

"If you ever want to leave this island and live a comfortable life again, you will become the demure, submissive wife required of you. Do I make myself clear?"

She scowls. "I'd rather rot in my cell than be married to you."

Staunton chuckles wryly. "You know, it is just the tiniest bit adorable that you still think you have any choice in the matter, but also the slightest bit irritating, seeing as how we don't have time to accommodate your stubbornness… Rhodes!"

Staunton grips Lily by the back of her neck and forces her to stand in front of him just as the door leading out the side of the great hall swings open and Lieutenant Rhodes shoves Tobias through.

Lily's eyes round and she gasps when she sees the state he's in. He's covered in bruises, and his tattered clothes are stained with both dried and fresh blood. Tobias's left eye is swollen shut and his right arm hangs limp at his side. She can tell immediately that it's either dislocated or broken.

She tries to run to him but Staunton's grip on her neck is tight and she's pulled backward. She looks at him pleadingly. He shoves her forward, releasing his hold on her a moment later. She rushes to Tobias as Rhodes does the same to him and he stumbles.

Lily catches her friend and helps lower him to the floor as her eyes fill with tears. Up close she can also see that some of Tobias's fingernails are missing on both hands .

"My friend," she gasps.

Tobias coughs, struggling to breath through his broken nose. "Miss. Lily." His voice is barely above a whisper. "I'm so sorry."

Lily sniffles. "You have absolutely nothing to be sorry for Tobias. I'm the one who's sorry, look what they've done to you because of me."

"Nonsense, it looks much worse than it feels." He laughs softly, attempting to soothe her, despite the state he's in. A few droplets of blood seep out the side of his mouth and Lily wipes them away with her thumb.

Lily turns her head to face Staunton. "Please, give him the medical attention he needs. He'll die without it."

Staunton saunters over, the joy he feels seeing Tobias in this state and its impact on Lily, radiating off him.

"Afraid it's not that simple, *dear*. You see, this prisoner helped you escape, which is a crime, and he's been punished accordingly. Like all other prisoners, if he dies, he dies."

He shrugs then turns to walk away, stopping when he feels a tug on the back of his coat.

"Please," Lily begs. Inside she's disgusted with herself for begging Staunton, but she sees no other way for Tobias to get what he needs. "I'll do anything."

Tobias's one good eye grows wide. "No, don't."

"Shut up you," Staunton snaps back at him before returning his gaze to Lily, who's still kneeling, stretched between supporting Tobias and keeping a hold of his coat tails, her eyes downcast.

"Kiss me," he demands.

Lily's stomach churns. She had a feeling he'd say something like this, but without medical aid, Tobias will die, so she slowly lowers Tobias's upper body to the floor, rises to her feet and locks eyes with Staunton. His anticipation and desire are clear as day. It only takes two steps for her to be in close enough proximity to kiss him.

Before she can talk herself out of it, Lily pushes up on her toes, locks lips with Staunton and closes her eyes. His lips are nothing like Jack's, they're thin and dry, and she can't wait to be parted from them. She allows the kiss to last a few seconds then slowly lowers herself back down until her feet are flat on the floor again.

When she opens her eyes, Staunton's are still closed. She watches as he inhales deeply, slowly licks his lips then opens his eyes.

Staunton's desires for Lily are running rampant within him. He has to have her, and soon. "Lieutenant Rhodes, bandage up the prisoner, then give him some fresh water and soup."

Rhodes salutes Staunton, picks Tobias up off the floor and roughly pulls him out the door they entered.

Lily looks after them before turning back to Staunton once the door closes. "Thank you," she whispers.

He doesn't respond, looking to Shryke instead. "How about it, Commander? Feels like the perfect afternoon for a wedding, don't you agree?"

A toothy smile spreads across Shryke's face. "I concur, Captain."

"What?" Lily demands. She knew a wedding would be planned, but absolutely did not expect one to take place today.

The two men ignore her while continuing their discussion. As a Commander, Shryke has the power to officiate and heartily agrees.

Within minutes Lily's released from the manacles and escorted to a room in one of the towers where one of the servants, a middle-aged woman named Tessa, waits with fresh bathwater and a new teal and gold dress draped over a chair.

"You have an hour," the guard states as he shuts and locks the door behind him.

Lily looks from the door to Tessa to the dress and

back again as her heart pounds and her breaths come in rapid succession.

She sinks to the floor.

Tessa hurries over and kneels beside her. "Lily, hey, Lily, look at me." She speaks in a calm tone, taking Lily's hands in her own.

Lily looks up at her, all of her emotions ready to burst forth.

"Do what I do, all right? Deep breath in."

Lily mimics Tessa.

"Good, now hold it a few seconds, then release slowly."

They do it together, then repeat the sequence again and again until Lily feels like she's returned to her body.

"Tessa, I can't," she begins after she's caught her breath.

"I can't imagine how you feel, but listen to me, if we don't get you ready, Shryke and Staunton will take it out on anyone who's ever been close to you here, especially Tobias since he helped you escape. He can't take much more."

Lily nods in agreement. "I saw him."

"None of this is fair, but you don't have a choice, none of us do in this wretched place. They hold all the power here."

Lily takes a few more deep breaths then stands. She knows Tessa's right, there is literally nothing she can do, so for her own sake, and that of the few people here she cares about, she'll marry Staunton, then spend her days plotting how to escape him and find her way back to Jack.

She turns her back to Tessa when she stands. "Can you please help me unlace and get out of this dress?"

~

Later that afternoon, the sound of Shryke's voice fades in and out of her head as Lily stands in front of Staunton, her hands trapped between his sweaty palms.

The weight of everything she's learned about Shryke and her mother, as well as her father, sits heavy on her heart.

She still has so many questions, but knows she'll never get the answers she now seeks given both her parents are dead and it's more clear than ever that Shryke's a maniac.

Until she can get away, this marriage to Staunton will be a new level of hell, she's sure of it.

"You may now kiss your bride," Shryke announces.

Staunton pulls Lily to him, pressing his mouth firmly against hers.

The small handful of guards in the hall clap. As she looks around, Lily notices there are fewer of them in here than usual, and they're more Staunton's men than Shryke's, but considering he's the one getting married, she figures some of them traded posts to be able to witness, especially given their loyalty to him.

"Well done." Shryke smiles as he shakes Staunton's hand.

"Thank you, Sir," Staunton replies before turning to

the wider room. "And now, a gift for my new wife. Just a small token of my love."

Lily cocks her head at him while he nods at Lieutenant Rhodes, who steps up next to the closest of Shryke's personal guard. Staunton quickly moves behind Shryke, draws his dagger, then slices it across the front of Shryke's throat.

She jumps back as the two men struggle; Staunton withdrawing the blade as Shryke claws at him in bewilderment.

The sound of commotion draws her attention and Lily watches in shock as Staunton's men quickly cut down Shryke's.

Shryke falls to the floor, blood spurting from the gash too quickly for him to do anything about it. His eyes dart from Staunton to Lily as he struggles to speak. Only a gurgling sound escapes him.

Staunton lifts one of Lily's hands to his lips, gently kissing it. "For you, my dear."

She looks at him, or, at least she thinks she is, but she doesn't quite feel like she's fully connected to her body. "What?" she mumbles.

He grins. "I believe the words you're looking for are thank you."

As the chaos in the hall ebbs, Shryke's body twitches its way into death's embrace, and while the flow of blood from his throat slows, Staunton addresses Rhodes. "Are the men in the other parts of the fort ready?" Staunton asks.

"Yes, Sir," Rhodes responds.

"Good, give the order. The sooner this asshole's men

are cleared out of here, the sooner we can really put our plan into motion to get the fuck off this island."

"With pleasure. Sir, if I may before I depart, are you sure we'll have enough men to manage the fort until our replacements arrive?"

Staunton scoffs. "Of course. The prisoners and slaves aren't going anywhere and have no idea what we're doing. We can manage with a skeleton crew until His Imperial Majesty's new Commander arrives. As far as anyone will ever know, Commander Shryke died of a sudden heart attack. We'll burn his body so no one will question it."

"Understood. And his men?"

"Put them in cells for now. We'll dispose of them when the time's right. Now, if you'll excuse me Rhodes, I'm a newly married man who's spent years waiting to spend some alone time with his new wife."

That statement snaps Lily back to reality and panic sets in at the prospect of being alone with Staunton now that Shryke's dead.

~

Lily strains and protests as Staunton pulls her up the flight of stairs toward their new living quarters. Fear oozes from every part of her body while she does everything in her power to prevent entry to the room.

Two guards follow close behind, eyes trained ahead, showing no reaction to what's happening in front of them.

Once inside, Staunton throws her to the floor then shuts the door behind him.

Lily lands hard, face toward the stone floor, then slowly rolls over and perches herself up on her elbows to look at him. "Please," she begs, eyes watering. "You can go be a Governor without having me as your wife. No one will try to stop you."

Staunton crouches beside her, his icy blue eyes the coldest she's ever seen them and full of malice, a menacing grin on his face. "Do you really think I give a shit about the governorship?"

He grabs her chin, lifting it in such a way that she has to look directly at him. "I couldn't care less. I've only ever wanted you. The governorship is just a perk." He gets closer, inhaling her scent.

Lily trembles. "W-w-why? You don't even know me."

Staunton grasps Lily by the shoulders and stands, forcing her up with him. "Oh, but I do. I've been watching you all these years Lily. You're strong, a fighter, not easily broken... and I crave that," he hisses. "Makes everything so much more interesting and fun."

Lily feels the confusion swirl in her mind. What man wants a woman who acts the way she's acted while here? Everything she'd been taught growing up suggested the opposite, that men want coy, demure, delicate women who know when to speak and when to keep their mouths shut, who have no opinions that differ from their husband's, and do whatever they're told.

Despite her disapproval and distaste of it, she used to be one of those women, before her time on Agrego forced her to be what he described. Only Jack appreciated the fighter in her, and he lived outside the bounds of the society she was born into and Staunton seemed to appreciate.

Staunton slowly moves his hands up Lily's shoulders until one rests at the base of her neck. He tightens his grip ever so slightly, but it's enough for Lily to notice.

As Staunton's grip continues to tighten, Lily realizes what he means. He wants someone he can control by any means necessary. The years of his treatment of her, the brutality of it all, plays out in her mind. Staunton wants to possess her. Shryke was a monster, but he'd set a hard boundary on how far Staunton was allowed to go with his punishments, and her maidenhead was off limits. With Shryke gone, there's no one to stop Staunton from doing what he so longed to do.

She knees him reflexively. Staunton groans, releasing his hold from around her throat and doubling over slightly. Lily quickly backs away, looking for something to defend herself with.

Staunton catches his breath and lets out a sinister chuckle before looking up at her. "You're going to fucking regret that." His eyes are wild now as he quickly shrugs his coat off and charges at her.

Lily darts to the left of the bed as Staunton slows his pace enough to not fall onto it. She runs for the door, but he's faster than she thought. As she pulls it open, his body hits hers hard, forcing the door closed again as he presses her against it, his front to her back, breathing heavily into her right ear. She struggles, trying to push back in the hopes that he stumbles, but he's too strong.

She's pinned.

While he has her up against the door, Staunton takes a key from his pocket, slips it into the keyhole and locks the door from the inside.

"No," Lily gasps.

He snarls in her ear before backing off her ever so slightly, then spins her around, pinning her back against the door. "You leave when I say you can, *wife*." Staunton slides the key into his pocket again and kisses Lily so hard it hurts.

She doesn't kiss him back, instead she starts pushing against him, trying to free herself. His height, weight and intensity are suffocating, and he's rough as he bites hard on her lower lip. She balls her hands into fists and tries to hit him, anything to get some space between them. His disgusting mouth on hers - where Jack's had rightfully been - turns her stomach.

As Staunton moves away slightly, she pulls her right fist back in the limited space she has and thrusts it forward, landing a punch right to Staunton's chest.

The blow catches him off guard but he doesn't retreat as far back as Lily had hoped. "Oh shit," she whispers.

When he looks at her, the fiery evil in his eyes sends a chill through her entire body and she instantly regrets what she's done.

Wordlessly, Staunton takes hold of some fabric on the front of Lily's dress and forcefully pulls her toward the bed. "So, you want to be rough, do you? Well, that's fine with me."

Lily fights against his grip as hard as she can. "No, please," she pleads. She's only ever been with Jack, something she'd wanted more than anything. The fear of what she knows is coming punches her in the gut.

When they reach the side of the bed, Staunton shoves her onto it face first. Lily has barely pushed herself up before she can feel him behind her rustling with the fabric of the dress.

He kicks her legs out from under her and she lands flat on the mattress again, legs dangling over the side, unable to find steady foot placement on the stone floor. She squirms, pushing back against the pressure of Staunton's hand pressing down on her upper back, and kicks her legs, trying her hardest to prevent him from truly positioning himself between them.

She pleads with him, but the more she resists, the stronger he seems to become.

Lily does all she can to get away, but her efforts are futile. She hears the buckle of his britches being undone, and her heart thunders even harder. Her muscles are beginning to give out from straining against the force Staunton's exerting over her.

Then, with a sudden thrust and an almost blinding pain, she feels him inside her. Her breath catches and a strained sound she's never made before escapes from her throat as tears flood her eyes.

Staunton repeats the motion, each thrust hurting more than the last. He grips her hair tightly, pulling her neck back at an uncomfortable angle that makes it feel as if it's difficult to breathe. He snarls vile things at her, goading her into continuing to fight back, which she initially does.

Eventually though, she no longer hears him. Her mind

goes blank and she stops fighting against him as he continues for what feels like an eternity.

As Lily stares blankly at the window across the room, she feels a warmth spread within her. Staunton collapses on top of her, breathless.

"Finally," he moans into her hair.

When he catches his breath, he rolls off of her and stands, buckling his pants as he does. He's silent while he dresses, taking a swig of ale from his goblet on the table.

After he's straightened out his shirt and uniform he leans in close to Lily, who's shaking uncontrollably on the bed. "Told you I'd make you scream again," he whispers with delight.

Without another word, he unlocks the door and leaves the room, closing, but not locking it, behind him.

Lily isn't sure how long she stays in the same position he left her in. Her body aches, both inside and out. The first time she was with Jack he'd warned her there would likely be some discomfort and soreness. Even though he'd been gentle he was right. This was so much worse.

By the time she decides to move, her legs are stiff and it takes some effort. She slowly rolls off the side of the bed, easing herself down to the floor, wincing.

She curls up on the cool stone floor, staring up at nothing in particular as she drifts in and out of her own mind, eventually falling asleep.

While she sleeps, Lily dreams of Jack and the dance they shared on the deck of the Savage Sea. She hears his voice in her head, whispering her name, the sense of comfort it brings envelopes her.

"Lily... Lily... Lily... Lily, please," stirs her awake. Tessa is kneeling next to her, her left hand resting on Lily's right shoulder.

Lily wipes the sleep from her eyes, and takes in the surroundings of the room. "Tessa?"

"Thank goodness," Tessa whispers. "I've been gently trying to wake you for a little while now. I thought I was going to have to call for Captain Staunton."

Lily's eyes widen as she looks around the room in fright. She takes hold of Tessa's hand and begins to sit up, struggling ever so slightly. When Tessa gets Lily standing they both look at the dried blood on the mattress.

"He hurt you," Tessa says softly. It's a clear statement, not a question.

Lily nods as the encounter rushes back to her and she starts to sob. "He's more of a demon than I ever realized. I thought if I could just make it long enough to get off this island I'd have a chance, but I can't stay here, I won't survive this, Tessa. He'll kill me," she chokes out.

Tessa wraps her arms around Lily. "Shh, shh." They rock side to side together. "What can I do?"

Lily takes a deep breath. She knows the risk and the likely answer but needs to ask anyway. "Is there any way you can get me out of the fort? I'll figure out getting to the docks myself."

Tessa frowns. "Oh Lily, he's never going to let you out of his or his men's sight now. He has too much at stake to take those risks with you."

"But... when he left earlier he didn't lock the door. If

I wasn't in such a state I could have gone…"

"There are guards right outside the door, I'd wager that's why he didn't lock it."

Lily blanches. "You mean… have they been out there the whole time? They heard what he was doing to me and just stayed out there?"

"I don't know about the whole time, but I'd assume so. Lily, their loyalty to Staunton runs deep, they'd never go against him. Besides, these men are so starved for a woman's touch. Raping slaves only fulfills so much of their needs. If it wouldn't likely result in their deaths, they may have been more apt to join in rather than help you."

Lily's breath catches in her throat. She knows Tessa's right, and she's not a stranger in this fort any longer, the pained cries of slaves in the night are more than familiar to her.

Tessa brushes some of Lily's matted hair away from her face. "How about we get you cleaned up?"

Lily wipes away the tears that have pooled along the corners of her eyes and nods. There's got to be something she can do to pacify Staunton.

~

While Tessa helps Lily, Jack stands at the bow of his ship, eyes trained on the horizon, mind on only one thing, getting to Lily as fast as possible.

At their current speed and as long as the wind doesn't

change, they should reach Agrego in two night's time.

Knox steps up behind him. "Captain?"

Jack remains facing forward. "What is it Knox?"

"Captain, Turner would like to continue discussing our plans before we get closer to Agrego. The crew is tough and loyal to you, they'll do what needs to be done, but the simple truth is that we're a single ship taking on a prison fort. We're at a significant disadvantage and need to plan for every contingency."

Jack clears his throat, nods once, then looks to the sky. "Hold on Lily," he whispers before turning to face Knox. "Yes, we need this to go perfectly."

He begins walking past Knox, who reaches out, putting his hand gently on Jack's shoulder, which stops him in his tracks.

"We'll get her," he states softly.

"Not saving her isn't an option," Jack replies. "Whatever it takes."

As he continues walking across the deck he can feel resistance in the air as the wind picks up and he pauses. This is exactly what they need to speed up their arrival to Agrego. "Thank you," he whispers. Jack looks up to Williams, who's at the helm. "Hold steady, Williams."

"Aye, Captain."

Jack pulls open the doors that lead to the crew quarters. "Everyone up on deck, now!" he calls down to them. The anger and fear he feels are consuming him and he needs to focus his restless energy. Once he hears men stirring he goes back up to the deck where the men already on duty have begun gathering.

Knox approaches from behind. "Captain?"

"Once the men are here, Knox."

Knox nods. "Wind's picked up."

"Yes," Jack replies flatly.

The crew gathers around him. He looks for Turner among them and addresses him directly once he finds him. "The most important thing is to get Lily out of there as quickly and safely as possible, and to send Shryke and Staunton straight to hell. We all know we're at a disadvantage, so, tell us how we succeed, Turner."

CHAPTER 11
HANGING BY A THREAD

A drizzle had been falling from the gray storm clouds swirling over Agrego since about an hour ago. Lily's leaning forward in the wash tub, arms wrapped around her knees as Tessa gently rubs a small washcloth across her back.

The dark purple hues of bruising have begun to reveal themselves after the past three days with Staunton. The ones on her hips and wrists are the most prominent from where he grips and holds her tightly.

She winces when Tessa passes the cloth over her right shoulder blade. Last night, Staunton had slammed it so hard into the bedpost that Lily was sure some bones had shattered based on the pain that exploded within her upon impact.

"Oop, I'm sorry," Tessa whispers.

There's a knock at the door. It's unlocked, always is when Staunton leaves, but the guards never just enter.

Tessa rises, goes to the door and opens it. "Yes?" she asks.

"The Captain requires her presence in the courtyard," the guard replies.

"Okay, she'll be down momentarily," Tessa responds evenly.

Once the door is closed again, Tessa returns to the tub and quickly finishes washing Lily's back. Lily towels herself off while Tessa pulls a pale blue dress from the wardrobe.

"How about this one?"

Lily glances up at the dress while she gently pats herself dry between her legs. The warm bath has helped some, but she's still sore after another rough night. "That's fine," she sighs.

Shortly after, two guards usher Lily and Tessa through the double doors leading out to the balcony overlooking the prison courtyard. The rain's begun to fall more steadily now, turning the courtyard itself into more of a mud pit than it usually is.

Staunton's seated under a small tent just big enough for his chair and some standing room beside him.

"You wanted to see me, Sir?" Lily asks.

Staunton grins. "Sir? Well, well, I have to say, it's only been a few days and my wife's attitude is already much improved."

Staunton rises and moves to stand beside Lily. He slips his arm around her waist, pulling her into him. "I told you it wouldn't take long. Still working on a few little hiccups, aren't we? However, I believe after today even those will disappear." He beams sardonically.

Lily keeps her face blank but she dreads what he may mean by " 'after today.' " Surely her sore shoulder from calling Staunton a sorry excuse for a man last night while she again attempted to fight him off before he fully overpowered her, was enough.

"Since it's clear you still haven't quite grasped the seriousness of your situation, I have a little surprise for you, my dear."

Lily looks nervous about what he could possibly mean, which sends a jolt of excitement through him.

Staunton brushes his lips against her ear. "Hopefully after this there will be no more fuck ups from you, darling."

Lily keeps her eyes trained straight ahead even though it feels like all her nerves are on fire. "What do you mean?"

Staunton steps to the balcony's railing. "Lieutenant Rhodes, if you please," he calls out.

Lily's gaze follows his to a door midway down the courtyard, just beyond the whipping post and gallows. Her heart drops to her stomach as she watches Lieutenant Rhodes march out ahead of two guards who drag an almost lifeless Tobias with them.

"No," she gasps, stepping out from under the tent to stand next to Staunton. "What is this? What are you doing?"

"You'll see."

She watches as Rhodes climbs up the steps of the gallows, then stands to the side while the guards haul Tobias up, propping him between them as they face the balcony.

Rhodes rolls open a small scroll. "By order of Captain Antony Staunton, interim Commander of His Imperial

Majesty's navy at Fort Agrego, prisoner Tobias Gillem is hereby sentenced to death by hanging for the crime of aiding a prisoner escape. Sentence to be carried out immediately." He rerolls the scroll.

Shocked, Lily turns to Staunton. "Wait, what is he talking about? This can't be, you promised you'd help him."

Staunton keeps his eyes focused on the platform as the guards pull the noose down around Tobias's neck. "I did," he responds flatly. "Then you disobeyed me last night, and now you need a reminder that your actions have consequences for others."

Lily grips his arm. "I understand, I won't do it again. Let him go. He paid for helping me escape, but I'm back now. You have me."

Staunton shakes her fingers off as he raises his other arm above his head. "Proceed," he instructs.

Lily's eyes widen in panic as she turns in time to see Rhodes pull the lever, releasing the door Tobias is standing on.

It's as if time suddenly slows down. Lily turns from Staunton and begins racing down the stairs leading from the balcony to the courtyard. She slips on the mud, coming out of one of her shoes, but continues running for the gallows, watching in horror as Tobias's body jerks around.

She calls out his name, which sounds distant to her own ears, as if coming from someone or somewhere else.

She's so focused on Tobias that she doesn't see the guard coming at her from the side. He catches her, wrapping his arms around her waist as they both slide on the mud in their struggle. He grips her tightly as she kicks and claws at him, desperate to break free.

The words "No!" and "Tobias!" continue to fall from her mouth in high-pitched shouts and screams as his body eventually goes completely limp.

As the realization that he's gone becomes reality, Lily drops to her knees and the guard loosens his hold. Sobs wrack through her body.

Staunton steps up beside her, using his chin to instruct the guard to leave. The joy he feels in seeing her so broken-hearted is evident on his face. "I told you to mind me like a good wife should. You didn't listen. Hopefully this is the last reminder you'll need. If not," he swivels to face the balcony, eyes falling on Tessa, "she'll be next."

Lily freezes then looks from Staunton to Tessa as horror engulfs her. "Please, stop," she sobs.

"What I do and don't do depends on you, Lily. Now get up and go wash, you're covered in mud."

Lily takes a steadying breath and rises. She bows her head toward Staunton but her eyes are fixed on Tobias's lifeless body swinging from the gallows.

"That's my good wife," Staunton teases.

Lily slowly makes her way back across the slippery yard, picking up her shoe along the way, then trudges up the steps to the balcony.

Tessa approaches, looping her arm around Lily's. She speaks softly but Lily doesn't respond, she just lets Tessa guide her back into the fort's tower and up to Staunton's chambers, shock having taken hold of her.

CHAPTER 12
BLADES IN THE DARKNESS

Lily sits on the floor of Staunton's chamber, legs criss-crossed, her head resting against the wall.

Within two week's time she learned of her mother's death, witnessed the result of her father's betrayal, was forced to marry Staunton, and watched helplessly today as Tobias was executed.

It was all too much, she was broken, and it feels like there's no fight left within her. In such a short amount of time, Staunton had succeeded where Shryke had failed. Lily was on the verge of becoming a husk of her former self, a former self already damaged from the previous three years.

The door to the chamber swings open and Staunton strides in. His eyes search the room, finding Lily sitting under the window.

He pauses, then smiles. "Oh, my darling wife, you look positively *awful*," he teases, moving toward her. He crouches down, placing one hand on top of her knees.

"Look at me," he orders.

She hesitates for the briefest of moments, but it's a moment too long for Staunton and Lily feels the sting of his open palm across her face.

"I said, look at me," he repeats softly, but somehow it sounds more threatening.

She does, silently absorbing the pain from his strike.

Staunton smirks. "Now, let's get you off this cold floor." He rises, offering her his hand.

She takes it and he pulls her upright.

"There, there," he scoffs, wiping the tears from her cheeks. "Let me see that beautiful face." Staunton slips his fingers under her chin and raises it upward quickly. "I'm sure prisoner Gillem's death was a shock to you, but I hope you now understand obedience better... yes?"

"Yes," Lily whispers, her voice unrecognizable to herself.

Over the last few days she's learned that when she puts up a fight it excites Staunton in the worst ways, making him violent. So, even though she can already sense what's about to happen, after what transpired earlier and his threat against Tessa, she feels there's no way to risk fighting back right now.

Lily begins to mentally prepare, imagining she's with Jack instead, and will let the memory of the nights they spent together fill every inch of her, blocking out everything about Staunton - his voice, his hands, his warm, stale breath.

"Wonderful! See? I knew you could be taught. Shryke was just doing it wrong this whole time. You're becoming the perfect wife for your future title."

Staunton kisses her gently on the forehead then pulls away slightly. She hates when he plays sweet, knowing the demon that lurks within.

He takes her hands, guiding her into the middle of the room. "Now, how about we continue trying for the son you're going to give me, hm?"

Staunton spins her around then comes up behind her, enveloping her in his arms. "There's no better way to honor the loss of a life, even one as insignificant as Gillem's, than by creating a new, more worthy one."

With the way he's pressed against her, Lily can feel him stiffening. Staunton uses one hand to guide her hips as he starts to sway from side to side. With the other, he caresses her breast over the top of her dress as he kisses along the length of her left shoulder, and up her neck to just below her earlobe.

She shudders.

"That's it," he whispers, misinterpreting her shudder of disgust for one of arousal. "Lift the hem of your dress," he instructs, gently pulling on her earlobe with his teeth.

She obeys, and as the hem rises above her knees, he continues using his own hips to make hers sway, slipping his newly free hand between her upper thighs.

Lily holds her breath as he starts teasing her with his fingers. Again, he mistakes it as a sign of pleasure and increases the speed of his movements, slipping his fingers inside her. Lily squeezes her eyes shut tightly, trying to dissociate.

Staunton stops what he's doing, removing his fingers

from inside her. Lily feels the fabric of her gown loosen as he undoes the lacing. The cool breeze from the window makes her shiver as her garment drops to the floor.

He turns her to face him and she opens her eyes as he does to avoid any wondering on his part as to why they were closed. She looks straight at him as his eyes wander across her exposed body. "You're mine" he goads, before taking off his own clothes, discarding them on the floor alongside her dress.

"I'll never be yours!" she mentally shouts.

"Shall we?" he asks, starting to back up toward the bed, forcing her to follow by holding onto her wrists.

Lily lowers herself into the same position he's put her in since the first time he raped her; her leaning over the bed, feet barely on the floor.

"No," he counters, pulling her upright and turning her to face him. "Get on your back."

"Oh fuck, he wants me to look at him while he does this?" is her immediate thought.

In an effort not to anger him, and to get this over with as quickly as possible, Lily does exactly what he says, without question.

Staunton positions himself on top of her and wastes no time. There's no more foreplay with him. Not that she'd ever complain, the sooner he's done, the better.

He pushes Lily's knees up then slips inside her.

Lily's body absorbs every horrible thrust, but despite this new attempt of his to connect with her, Lily doesn't look at him. Her eyes are glued to the ceiling as she lets her mind wander. Like the times before, she replaces

Staunton with Jack. Not that it matters visually, Staunton's head is down by her left ear, his hot breath warming that small area of her skin.

As she gets lost in the memories of those nights on the Savage Sea with Jack, she remembers every detail, including the way she moaned his name and what it did to him.

She whispers his name again in her mind. This time he doesn't respond.

Instead there's quiet and another voice replaces his. "What did you say?"

Lily's eyes fly open and she's face to face with Staunton, who's perched on top of her. Panic rises within her. Had she said Jack's name aloud? No, she couldn't have, she'd been so careful. Right?

"What the fuck did you just say?" he asks again, each word delivered with pointed precision.

Lily hesitates, not knowing how to respond.

Staunton takes hold of each of her wrists, pressing them hard into the mattress.

She winces. "You're hurting me," she cries out.

Staunton's eyes are ablaze. "You said 'Jack,' " he hisses, holding her wrists tighter, taking in the terrified look on her face. "Did you let that pirate scum fuck you?" he demands.

When she doesn't respond, he pushes off her, then climbs out of the bed.

Lily lays there, stiff, unsure what to do as Staunton begins to pace.

"I'm a dead woman."

It's almost as if he's heard her because the next thing

she knows, Staunton's dragging her off the bed, forcing her to stand naked in front of him.

He asks the question again, but Lily still doesn't answer.

"I swear, if you don't fucking answer me..."

The anger she's been pushing down explodes to the surface, along with the realization that nothing matters anymore. Would it really be so bad if he actually killed her? At least she'd be free from his torture. "Yes, I let him fuck me!" she yells. "And I fucked him right back you repulsive, vile piece of shit!"

Lily braces for his strike, only it doesn't come.

Staunton just stands there for a few moments before he quickly dresses and leaves without another word.

Lily knows better than to feel any sense of relief though. He may not have said anything, but the glare he gave her before departing may have been one of the most unsettling things he's ever done, and that's saying a lot.

She pulls her discarded chemise down over her head, then stands by the window looking out at the sea, waiting for Staunton to come back and hopefully end this miserable life of hers.

~

As dusk approaches, Staunton still hasn't returned. Lily sits by the fire in her chemise, eyes staring but not seeing as she's so lost in thought.

Suddenly, the door opens and she snaps her head in its direction, expecting to see Staunton barge through. Only, it's not him, it's the two guards who were stationed outside the door. Lily jumps up from the chair, covering her chest with her arms as she does.

Without uttering a single word, the two guards approach. Each loops an arm under hers and begin walking toward the door. Her questions about what they're doing go unanswered.

As they forcefully guide her through the halls of the fort, she begins to recognize where they are. She hasn't been down to this part of the prison in three years, not since the night Shryke had the witch take her memories.

The level of fear at that possibly happening again surges within her and Lily really attempts to struggle against their hold as the door to the room comes into view.

Despite her best efforts, they're just too strong for her. One reaches forward, turns the doorknob, then gives the door a bit of a push. They all wait as it slowly creaks open, revealing dim lighting from within. The guards shove Lily through the door before pulling it closed behind them and taking their respective posts in the hallway outside.

Lily stumbles forward from the force of their shove, landing on her right hip and both wrists as they absorb the impact of her fall. With her head and eyes cast downward, she immediately begins to tremble as the sound of boots hitting the stone floor echoes off the walls. Within moments, a pair of buffed up, navy-issued ones enter her limited field of vision.

"Stand up," Staunton instructs in a low, threatening tone.

Lily shakes her head vigorously as tears well in her eyes.

"I said, 'stand up,' " he repeats, this time roughly grabbing her by the hair and yanking upward.

"Aagh!" Lily immediately covers his hand with her own, hoping for some leverage to loosen his grip, but there is none.

She quickly gets to her feet and Staunton releases her. With the sound of her heart pounding in her ears, Lily surveys the room. The light she'd seen when the guard opened the door was coming from the lit fireplace, where some sort of liquid inside a small cauldron boils and steams. A table of supplies sits off to the side with empty glass vials strewn about.

As she continues scanning the room, Lily notices that the long table she'd been strapped to three years ago has been pushed against the far wall, and a large wooden chair replaces it in the center of the room.

"Sit down," Staunton hisses.

Lily barely gets out "What? I," before he forces her over to the chair and shoves her down onto the seat. She immediately notices the open straps on the armrests and looks to Staunton pleadingly. "What are you doing? Antony, please," she cries out as he uses his body weight to hold her in place, forcing her left arm through the strap.

"Oh, it's Antony now, is it? " he asks mockingly as he repositions himself to do the same to her right arm. "Am I no longer a vile piece of shit?"

Lily cringes at the callback to earlier. He always has been and always will be a vile piece of shit, but allowing her emotions to get the best of her and actually calling him one was now proving to be a horrible mistake.

Staunton finishes strapping each of her ankles to their respective chair legs, then steps back to take in the sight of her in this vulnerable state, absolutely at his mercy. He waits for her to stop straining against the straps before deigning to speak again.

"I'm supremely disappointed and disgusted by you," he announces. "To think that my pure, high-born wife allowed a dirty pirate of all things, to use her body. Well, it makes me sick."

Lily straightens her spine against the back of the chair as he slowly approaches.

He places his hands on the front part of the armrests, lowering his face until it's level with hers. "Now, you're going to tell me everything you know about Jack Teague and his crew."

Lily frowns as her eyes grow wide. "Never," she hisses. "Just kill me now because you'll get nothing from me."

Staunton quickly wraps one of his hands around her throat and exerts just enough pressure to impact her breathing, but not stop it. "Kill you? Oh, you poor, dumb thing. I would never kill you... at least, not yet."

"I won't help you," she gasps.

Staunton releases her throat and Lily coughs as she tries to gulp down some air.

A thin-lipped smile spreads across his face. "You will. You see, Lily, I'm going to do one of the things I enjoy doing to you most, but I have to make sure you don't die on me, because, well, that just won't help my plan. Thankfully, our powerful friend here reminded me that she has just the thing to ensure you don't slip away permanently."

Lily turns her head in the direction he's pointing as the witch from three years ago materializes out of the shadows, a large vial of brown liquid in her hand.

"What are you…" Lily doesn't have a chance to finish asking the question before Staunton backhands her hard across the face. The immediate pain in her cheek radiates up behind her eye, the force of the blow causing her head to slam into the back of the chair.

He holds out his hand and the witch places the vial in it. Staunton uncorks it then pushes Lily's head up so he can pour some into her mouth.

"Not too much," the witch reminds him.

Staunton grunts in response.

As the liquid slides down her throat, Lily notices that the pain in her cheek and back of her head lessen.

"See?" Staunton asks while putting the cork back in the vial. "Now, tell me about the pirate."

Lily's mind swirls with what this elixir means. Could he actually torture her to the brink of death and pull her back as many times as he wants?

Jack had done so much for her and she loved him. The thought of living while any piece of information about him or his crew, no matter how small, was used to find them, was unfathomable.

Lily takes a deep breath, closes her eyes, then looks straight at Staunton when she opens them. "Go to hell," she declares, hoping her tone of defiance is stronger than it feels.

Staunton's face contorts with a look of disbelief and confusion. "Excuse me?"

"You heard me, vile piece of shit. You'll get nothing from me."

Staunton hands the vial back to the witch before getting in Lily's face again. Her resolve's clear, but considering he hasn't even really begun, he's sure it won't take long to break it, and her. "We'll see about that, *my dear.*"

Four hours later, blood drips from Lily's mouth, running down her chin and onto the chemise. A gash along her right bicep bleeds freely while the two broken fingers on her left hand hang awkwardly. She's passed out from the pain and Staunton has yet to give her another sip of the elixir.

"Be careful where you bruise her," the witch warns. "The wounds will heal quickly, but they'll leave scars, just as they would if they healed on their own."

"So what?" he asks as he takes a swig of mead from his goblet. "Why do you care?"

The witch's tone remains flat and even. "I care not, but if you expect her to be presentable as your wife, if she survives this, visible scars will cause speculation."

He sighs, knowing she's right. Luckily, what he's done so far can easily be hidden under clothing, but he'll have to be careful as he continues.

Staunton pours some elixir down Lily's throat and she gasps as she regains consciousness.

"Welcome back," he announces as she slowly rolls her

head to relieve some of the stiffness. Lily looks down at her fingers, groaning and letting out an "Aghhh," through gritted teeth as the broken bones snap back into place.

"This can all end, just tell me about the fucking pirate."

"Like what?" she gasps.

"Let's start with an easy one. Where do they call home?"

Lily rests her head against the back of the chair. "I don't know." Jack had told her about the island of Havara, where most of the crew called home, but not exactly where it was located. Since she'd never heard of it before and he hadn't provided its location, it wasn't technically a lie.

Staunton crouches down in front of her, resting the tip of his dagger on the top of her thigh; not hard enough to draw blood, but enough to tell her that with just a bit more force, it would happen. "You're lying."

Lily shrugs her shoulders. "You'll never know."

Staunton shakes his head slowly. "All right." He glances at the placement of his dagger. "You know, you have a beautiful thigh, it'd be a shame to keep hiding it underneath that chemise."

In one quick motion, Staunton slices at the fabric, exposing the flesh from Lily's upper thigh to just below her knee.

He then lightly traces the dagger along her skin, which causes her to gulp. "What shall I do now?"

Lily tenses as she watches the muscle in her upper thigh twitch. Staunton pauses mid-thigh, then takes a deep breath, soaking in the joy he feels from Lily's high-pitched scream as he forces the tip of the blade through her skin.

Her chest heaves as the corners of her vision become blurry, but Lily manages to hold onto consciousness. When Staunton removes the blade, she watches as her blood bubbles at the skin's surface before sliding down her inner thigh and disappearing below the fabric of her chemise.

"Something to say?" he asks.

Lily's body trembles as adrenaline courses through it. She slowly looks up at him, determined to not give in. "Fuck you," is all she says before letting her body slump in the chair.

Staunton curses then kicks over the stool he'd been using to rest on. He looks at the witch. "Don't give her any elixir unless she's on the verge of dying. I'll be back." With that, he spins on his heels, slamming the door shut behind him.

Lily can hear him speaking to the guards in the hall but his voice is low and muffled. The sound of his footfalls on the stone floor fade away and she lets out a long exhale. There's no concept of time in this windowless room so she has no idea how long she's been down here.

The door to the room opens and the two guards enter, one with an ankle manacle draped over his arm. Like upstairs, they unhook Lily from the chair without speaking, then carry her over to a corner of the room. A trail of blood marks her path. They attach one end of the manacle to the wall, the other around her right leg, then depart, neither with the courage to look her in the eyes once.

"Cowards!" She calls after them as the door latches closed behind them, before looking to the witch, who's stirring whatever's in the little cauldron over the fire.

"Why do you help him?" Lily asks, and the witch pauses, but doesn't turn to face her. Lily sniffles. "Whatever happened to maintaining the balance and not interfering beyond that?"

The witch's cloudy eyes find Lily's, but still she says nothing.

Tears sting the corners of Lily's eyes as she presses on. "I met one of your sister witches. Eudora? What would she say if she saw you now?"

The witch slowly moves around the table toward Lily, but doesn't go further than that. "Careful, fragile one. Save your energy and anger for the one you really hate."

"I hate you both," Lily bites back.

The witch lets out a "Hm," then goes back to the cauldron. "Without my elixir, you'd be dead by now."

"Exactly. Why do you think I hate you? You're helping to keep me alive."

The witch nods. "Death would be a shame."

"Death would be freedom," Lily counters.

She offers no response.

Eventually, Lily lowers her whole body onto the cold stone, letting exhaustion claim her.

~

While Lily drifts between sleep and semi-consciousness, Jack jumps from one of the longboats onto the shore as the others are guided in beside him.

That increased gusting of the wind the other night had really helped their speed, and they'd made it to the far side of the island under the cover of night.

As the fourth and final longboat comes to a stop down the line and the men climb out, rearming themselves as they do, Jack studies the beachhead. Turner was right, there's plenty of coverage for them to follow the smaller cliffs until they get closer to the fort, then commence the climb up to one of the outer posts ahead of their attack.

He looks further down the beach, the glow from the fort's towers drawing his gaze. "Hold on Lily." His voice is barely above a whisper, as his eyes narrow in determination.

Turner and Vane step up behind him. Jack and Vane haven't spoken since the incident on deck, but Jack knows his strongest crew member will do exactly what's expected of him.

"Ready Captain," Vane announces, his two swords strapped criss-cross along his bare back. He has daggers hooked around his waist, each at a perfect, easy to grab angle.

Jack turns around to look at his assembled crew. "The Savage Sea?" he asks.

"On its way toward the bay. Tate knows to drop anchor behind the cliffs until we give them the signal, then they'll engage from the water," Turner responds.

"Good." Jack signals for the men to gather as closely as possible so he can keep his voice low. They're not expecting patrols this far out but better to be overly cautious than even the least bit reckless. "Remember, we offer no quarter or mercy until after we locate Lily."

"What about slaves and prisoners?" Singleton asks.

Turner looks at him, expression serious. "Any slaves or prisoners willing to fight with us are free to do so. We can certainly use their help and I imagine they'll be more than willing to get revenge against Shryke, Staunton, and their men."

Jack nods. "Exactly. Help free and outfit them with whatever weapons you can find, then keep pushing toward the inner parts of the fort. The group heading for the defensive outpost will split from the rest of us when we reach the top of the cliffs. Listen for their warning shot from the cannon, that's what will signal Tate to begin the bombardment from the water."

The men nod before beginning their trek across the sand toward the lowest part of the cliffs.

They stealthily ascend, waiting patiently as the first group reaches the top and begins spreading out, looking for sentries and patrols. A series of whistles alerts each additional group that it's safe to get up over the ridge and seek cover among the trees and brush.

When the last of the crew are pulled over the ridgeline they begin to split up, with the small group assigned to take the defensive post nearest the bay breaking away first.

As Jack leads the others toward the fort, they encounter their first patrol of two men. Using the shadows to their advantage, Turner and Vane are able to sneak up behind each of them, catching them off guard.

Jack paces in front of the two guards as their outer coats are stripped away. "Where are they keeping the girl?" he demands.

"We're not telling you shit," one of them spits back.

Jack shrugs. "Fine by me."

He nods to Vane who slits the throat of the one who talked back as the other begins to tremble.

Once the body of the one with the slit throat finishes twitching, Jack rests his elbows on his knees in front of the remaining one, dagger held casually in his palm. "You sure you don't have anything to say?"

The soldier gulps. He's a younger guy, which Jack hopes will work to his advantage; someone who doesn't know any better and wants to live.

"A-a-are you talking about Governor Mearas's daughter?" he stutters out.

"Yes."

"S-she's here."

Jack and the crew chuckle. "We know she's here. I need a more exact location. Savvy?"

The guard swallows hard. "I d-don't know where she is e-exactly, but it'd be somewhere in the inner f-fort."

Jack cocks his head. "Not the prison?"

"N-no. Why would C-Captain Staunton's wife be in the prison?"

The dagger falls from Jack's hand in surprise. "What did you say?"

"They're married. Commander S-Shryke officiated the wedding right before he had a h-heart attack."

A slight ringing begins in Jack's ears at this news. Married? Lily would never agree to that. He rises, his gaze quickly moving to the fort as the thought of her being in more trouble than anticipated crosses his mind.

Without prompting, Vane slits the guard's throat as Turner walks over to Jack.

"Shryke's dead," is all he says.

"Just one less asshole to kill," Jack responds flatly. He looks to the men, who wait expectantly for his next order. "With Shryke dead, we can assume Staunton's in charge. The plan remains the same."

The crew falls in line as they push on toward the lower outer wall of the fort. They need to get inside before the cannon is fired, alerting Staunton to their presence.

Looks like there's a bit of luck on their side. After encountering another patrol, they learn that one of the outer doors only has a single guard stationed behind it due to its location. The crew stands out of sight as George, the youngest and one who looks the least like a pirate, puts on the outer coat of the newest dead guard and approaches the door.

He knocks twice, entering slowly as the door opens. Keeping his head down, he trips as he enters, distracting the one guard just long enough for Jack to follow him through the door. Covering the guard's mouth with one hand and dragging his knife across the man's throat with the other, Jack makes quick work of the killing.

As the crew files in, they prop the guard up on his little stool, angling his head in a way that you'd have to get really close with a torch to notice that his throat's been slit. Jack unhooks the keys from the man's belt before they all continue down the dimly lit corridor toward the cells.

When they reach a staircase, Jack instructs a large contingent of the men to follow him up so they can start searching the upper floors, while Vane and a few others remain behind to scour the dungeons for slaves and prisoners.

~

The kick to her ribs comes hard and swift. Lily's ripped from her sleep by the force of it. She's too delirious from pain and unaware of her surroundings to prevent the side of her head from smacking against the floor, and the warmth of fresh blood spreads along the side of her forehead as ringing permeates her ears.

"Rise and shine," Staunton announces with mock excitement as he unlocks her ankle manacle.

She rolls onto her back as she repeatedly gasps, struggling to breathe.

Staunton notices that the hole in her thigh has scarred over. "I thought I told you not to give her elixir unless she was practically dead," he calls over to the witch.

The witch simply shrugs then goes back to grinding herbs.

Lily still doesn't have the wherewithal to comprehend what's happening, her sole focus is on getting enough air into her lungs, which is currently proving difficult as she senses a few of her ribs are definitely cracked.

Staunton narrows his eyes at the witch but decides it's not worth his time. Instead, he hovers over Lily. "I know it's not the gentlemanly thing to say, but you've looked better." He pauses briefly before continuing. "In fact, I think one of your best looks was when that beautiful back of yours was exposed to me for the first time so I could decorate it with the whip. How about it? Should we give that another try? Or are you ready to cooperate?"

Lily wheezes, blinking her eyes rapidly, her mouth open as if she wants to say something.

Staunton bends at his knees. "What's that, *dear?* I didn't quite catch it."

She collects as much oxygen as her lungs will allow, then forces her eyes to focus on him. "You're not a man," she responds with as much venom and bite as she can muster in this moment.

"The hell did you just say to me?!" he bellows.

Lily coughs and the tightness it produces in her chest overwhelms her. "You heard me," she croaks out.

Without another word, Staunton wraps his hand around Lily's wrist and begins dragging her across the floor, back toward the chair. Lily groans while he does. As she's now all too aware, the elixir may heal wounds, but the pain and tenderness the injuries cause still exist, and her body's feeling the repercussions of every blow she's taken since she was thrown in here.

Once in front of the chair, Staunton releases her and she immediately slumps forward. Lily listens as he unbuckles his belt, but her eyes stay focused on the witch, shooting daggers at her.

The witch drops some herbs into her cauldron and gives it a stir, ignoring Lily's glare.

"Almost ready?" Staunton asks.

The witch nods once.

"Good." He swings and the leather belt makes contact against Lily's back.

Her body sways from the inertia of the hit, and an "Mmph" escapes her, but she doesn't attempt to get away. Truth be told, it's unlikely she could even if she tried.

Right as Staunton draws his arm back to strike again, the sound of a distant cannon firing reverberates through the walls. He pauses, questioning whether he truly heard it. Just as he's about to decide that it was only his imagination, it sounds again and the two guards come through the door.

"Sir," one says as soon as he steps through. "We have a problem."

"I can hear that," he replies with annoyance as he lowers his hand holding the belt to his side. "What is it?"

As the guard is about to say he's unsure, another runs toward them from down the hall. "Captain! One of our defensive posts is firing their cannon at our walls and there's a ship in the harbour doing the same!"

It only takes a few seconds for Staunton to put the pieces together. He swivels his head in a snake-like manner to look at Lily. "He's here."

He stalks toward her, the guards following close behind. "Get her in the chair," he orders as he crosses the room, quickly closing the distance between him and the witch. "How much longer?" he asks.

She looks down at the cauldron as a bubble pops and the liquid turns black. "It's ready."

"Perfect." He makes his way back to the chair, stopping in front of Lily as the guards finish tying her arms. "Looks like tonight's my lucky night. No need for me to wait any longer for you to break, the pirate's come to me."

Lily struggles to lift her head but she manages to do so as a third round of cannon fire sounds. "No," she moans weakly. She's already endured so much, the thought of it all being in vain sends a wave of nausea washing over her.

"Don't worry," Staunton continues. "I won't kill him until after you've seen each other. You see, I have a better idea than what I originally planned. That little potion that's been brewing while you've been in here? It's your old friend, the memory eraser. At first, I was just going to give it to you when I got bored of this. But now? Now I'm going to make you forget him while you're looking into his eyes."

Lily's mouth drops open slightly as Staunton walks toward the door.

"Keep an eye on her until I return. You've almost earned your freedom," he announces to the witch before slamming the door shut behind him.

"No, no, no," Lily mumbles as she fights through the pain, straining as much as she can against her bonds. Through a shaky breath she yells for Staunton to come back then curses at the witch for continuing to do nothing.

Vane and two members or the crew watch from the shadows of a side hallway as Staunton and the guards run to the nearest set of stairs, and up toward the melee that's started above. They'd found six cells of slaves and prisoners who were more than willing to help fight their way out of here, which is exactly what they started doing.

"Let's go," Vane orders gruffly, and the three of them creep down the hall to where they'd just seen Staunton.

In the room, Lily whimpers as the witch forces her head back. She's so overcome with pain and worry that she doesn't realize it's the healing elixir that the witch is trying to pour down her throat, not the memory eraser.

"You must drink. Do so for what's inside," the witch instructs in a calm but authoritative voice.

" 'What's inside?' " Lily asks, unsure what the witch means.

The witch seizes the opportunity and pours some of the elixir into Lily's mouth, placing her hand over it so Lily can't spit it out.

The door crashes open and they both startle at the sound. Lily tenses until she realizes it's Vane standing there.

His eyes search the room, falling on the scene of the two women almost immediately. He registers Lily's bloodstained face, chemise and exposed bruises, and his eyes narrow on the old witch. She turns to face him, and in the moment it takes for her to do so, he palms one of his thinner blades then throws it.

The blade hits its intended target, lodging just above

her heart. She stumbles backward then falls to her knees as the vial of healing elixir shatters on the floor.

"Vane," Lily calls weakly.

He rushes over to the chair and unbinds her hands as the other two pirates keep their eyes on the hallway.

"I didn't tell him anything," she announces softly as her body relaxes into the chair.

Vane had misjudged her before, and it was time to make up for it, for his Captain's sake. He crouches in front of Lily, assessing both her open and healed wounds. The side of his jaw slackens a little as he watches the cut on her forehead miraculously heal and scar over. "Of course you didn't," he begins. "You belong to the Savage Sea, we're not easily broken."

They offer each other a small smile of respect and understanding before Vane slips his massive hand behind Lily to help her out of the chair. It's a slow process and she winces as her body continues to heal. It's clear to him that he must shoulder most of her weight if they're going to get out of here quickly.

The witch spits some blood from her mouth as she lays on the floor. She looks up at Lily. "You were right, death is freedom." A hollow breath leaves her body and she goes limp.

Lily and Vane watch in awe as the body of the gnarled old woman fades to that of a young one who looks almost identical to Eudora, before it disintegrates into dust.

There are so many questions Lily wishes she could ask about what she's just witnessed, but she looks to Vane and simply says, "Staunton knows you're here. Where's

Jack?"

He holds her gently but close. "Come on, getting you out of here is our top priority. We'll find Jack."

The four of them make their way to the door, Lily limping slowly, relying on Vane's support.

They cross the threshold and start heading down the hall.

She doesn't look back.

CHAPTER 13
THE HEART OF THE CORSAIR

Jack swings his sword, catching the guard off balance. He brings his leg up and thrusts forward, kicking the man in the stomach, then watches as he tumbles backward down the stairs.

Jack spins, continuing his way up the tower to where he believes Staunton's sleeping quarters are located, and hopefully Lily as well.

When he arrives at the top of the staircase, he kicks in the first door he comes to, which opens up into what's clearly the room of a senior officer. He looks around quickly and has just decided to leave when he spots what appears like a discarded dress on the floor between the far wall and the bed.

As he picks up the garment, he spots slight movement out of the corner of his eye and turns quickly to face it. He pauses when he realizes it's a scared woman clinging to the corner of the bed, trying to back herself into the wall.

Jack lowers his blade. "I'm not going to hurt you," he says calmly, then holds up the dress to her. "Who does this belong to?"

Tessa continues to shake and doesn't answer.

"Lily? Does this dress belong to Lily?"

She nods.

He drops the dress and goes to Tessa, kneeling in front of her. "Where is she? Please, tell me."

Tessa's about to answer when commotion out in the hall snaps both of their heads in the direction of the door just in time to watch Staunton and the two guards from the dungeons barge in.

Jack rises quickly, lifting his blade. "Where is she?" he demands with a slight growl as Staunton and the two guards spread out on the opposite side of the room, blocking the door.

"If I told you she was dead?" Staunton snivels.

"I wouldn't believe you," Jack replies, flatly.

"Well, you're dead to her. Or will be, shortly."

Jack's jaw tenses. "What the fuck did you do?"

Staunton grimaces. "Nothing yet. At least, not to her mind. Her body, however? Let's just say it's seen better days."

Jack's nostrils flare, but he doesn't respond. He knows Staunton's trying to distract him as the two guards continue to slowly make their way closer around the outer edges of the chamber, but he's been clocking and tracking their movements the entire time.

"I knew this time would come, but I'll be honest, I was hoping I'd be governor of Mearas by then."

Jack shrugs. "The best laid plans. Now, I'll only ask

once more, where is she?"

"My wife's resting comfortably, or rather, uncomfortably I'm afraid, somewhere else. The next time you see her you'll be on your knees, watching helplessly as she forgets you in real time. Get him," Staunton instructs the guards.

They both lunge for Jack, but he's still just a little too far out of their reach, so it's easy for him to use their over-stretched arms against them. The three of them clash, the sound of their swords making contacts echoing off the walls.

With one soldier's neck tucked under his armpit, Jack shoves his dagger up through the man's chin then releases him, letting gravity pull him down. The other guard recovers from his half kneel position quickly and swings wildly. The exaggeration of the move provides the opening Jack needs and he slashes his sword across the man's exposed neck.

Jack's head tilts tauntingly at Staunton, goading him to engage.

Just as Staunton's about to, Tessa's trembling voice breaks the strained silence. "The dungeons," she calls out.

Staunton gives her a deadly look as Jack maintains his position.

"Thank you," he replies, hoping she can hear the gratitude in his voice. He can't wait any longer for Staunton to make his move and forces his hand.

Their blades clash like thunder, and it only takes a few moves for Jack to acknowledge that they're pretty evenly matched and he needs to change up his strategy. As their duel moves back out into the hallway, Jack pushes Staunton toward the stairwell, hoping to gain the high ground. Despite Staunton's best efforts, he's unable to change direction and finds himself at the precipice of the stairs.

In an act of desperation, he swings somewhat wildly and the very top of his blade catches a small area of Jack's lower abdomen. Jack grunts at the sting and glances down, placing his free palm over it. Thankfully, it only takes moments for him to realize the wound's superficial.

"Ah, he bleeds," Staunton taunts, watching as Jack pulls his hand away.

Jack smirks. "Don't worry, you will too. That's a promise." He gets himself back into position, then uses his sword to distract Staunton while he pulls one of his smaller, more lightweight daggers from around his waist. Jack flicks it and watches as it careens past Staunton, nicking him along the side of his neck as it goes.

Staunton's eyes widen in shock and his hand flies up to his neck.

Jack spreads his arms wide and bows slightly from his middle. "Told you," he quips. "Don't worry, it's not fatal. I'm not the one who should kill you, I'll leave that honor to Lily."

He doesn't give Staunton the opportunity to respond. He re-engages immediately, and as he does, Staunton's forced to take a step down, allowing Jack to gain the upper hand.

The steel of their swords sing as they are clashed

against each other and driven along the stone walls that encase the two men, creating brief sparks from the friction. As they descend the stairs, the sounds of the fighting in the great hall reach their ears, a symphony of shouts, metal on metal, and the occasional pistol firing.

As Jack and Staunton step onto the final landing before the last set of stairs, Staunton manages to loop his arm between Jack's, tangling them and their swords. He uses that leverage to shove Jack into the wall, their angry and determined faces almost touching.

"How does it feel?" Staunton asks through gritted teeth. "Knowing we've both enjoyed her?"

Jack's face drops briefly.

"I must confess, the thought of you having had her at all turned my stomach. But, I treasured her screams nonetheless." He's hoping to elicit enough anger in Jack that he becomes careless, even briefly, allowing Staunton to take control of this fight.

Unfortunately for Staunton, rage, despair and the animal within Jack, the one he nurtured in order to kill his father, burst forth. Jack leverages the sole of his left foot against the wall and pushes off as hard as he can. The two of them tumble down the last section of stairs, crashing hard on the floor, untangling from one another when they land.

Staunton rolls away, spitting some blood and a tooth from his mouth as he does. He stops on his stomach, spits once more then glances over to Jack, who's a few feet away on his back and rubbing his fingers along the side of his head. Staunton then looks up and through the open arches into the great hall, confronted by the chaos within. He hadn't realized prisoners and slaves were released, and his men were being overpowered.

He realizes that he can use the confusion to his advantage though, so he takes a deep, steadying breath and rises, grunting as he does. He enters the hall, disappearing into the crowd.

Jack tracks his movement, following suit.

~

The clanging of metal and shouting in the great hall grows louder as Vane's group approaches. Vane's hesitant to bring Lily so close to the fighting, but it's the most likely place Jack will be and he needs his Captain to know that he's done his duty and Lily's safe.

As their little group is about to cross an open hallway, six soldiers appear, blocking their path. Vane perches the still bruised and hurting Lily against the wall before he and his fellow crewmates engage them. When two have been disposed of and there's a clear path for her to get through, he turns to Lily.

"Go!" he shouts.

Lily struggles to push herself off the wall but manages it, then stumbles forward and past the group.

"Find Jack," Vane calls after her as she approaches the entrance to the great hall, the epicenter of the confrontation.

Lily keeps low, sticking to the outskirts of the hall, trying desperately to get to Jack, who's in the process of fighting off two soldiers. She comes upon the dead body of one of Staunton's men, pistol still in hand, eyes void of any life. She takes the pistol from his loose grip and checks it, there's still a projectile inside.

The sound of an angry yell draws her attention in time to see Staunton slice through an Agrego prisoner.

As the man drops to his knees, she watches Staunton look up, eyes fixed on Jack, who's still currently engaged in combat with two of his men. Staunton pulls the empty pistol from his hip and begins to reload.

"No," she gasps, then stands, leaving the miniscule safety of the shadows as she fiddles with the pistol in her own hand.

Time slows as nausea grips her, but she fights it and begins making her way through the fighting, eyes darting between Jack and Staunton.

Jack's cut down one of the soldiers he's been parrying with, but is still locked with the other and has no idea Staunton's setting up for a shot.

Staunton catches sight of Lily and his rage boils over. She was his now and the time had come to break her forever. Forgetting the memory eraser, he focuses back on finishing his pistol's reload and takes aim at Jack.

Staunton lets out a slow exhale and fires as he whispers "She's mine."

Jack finishes swinging his blade across the chest of the remaining soldier, then spins around to face the direction of the shot. He's met by the back of a head of red curls and a shout of "No!"

Lily stumbles backward into him as Staunton's projectile rips into her upper abdomen, just below her ribs. She looks up into Jack's wide eyes, her breath immediately laboring as she attempts to hand him the pistol.

"Don't miss," she instructs softly.

With his left arm stabilizing Lily's body, Jack keeps the pistol in her hand, wraps his fingers around hers and raises it, taking aim at a stunned-looking Staunton. He pulls the trigger and the pistol fires, the projectile striking the Captain at the base of his throat before Staunton can even register what's happened.

Activity in the hall slowly ceases as Staunton's body falls to the floor, eyes frozen open in shock. Jack lowers down a slumping Lily, his eyes never leaving hers.

"You came for me," Lily gasps, blood continuing to seep through her already torn, tattered and bloody chemise.

"Of course I came," Jack replies, attempting to assess her newest injury. "Why did you do that?" he begs.

Lily smiles slightly. "He had the drop on you."

Jack quickly removes his shirt then presses down on the fresh wound in an attempt to slow the bleeding. He also conducts a quick assessment of all the freshly healed injuries he can see, understanding immediately what Staunton meant when he'd commented on the state of Lily's body.

"You're hurt," she observes, seeing the small gash on his stomach from Staunton's blade.

He guffaws, trying to remain calm. This wasn't supposed to happen. "What, this? Don't even feel it."

She laughs briefly before registering the silence in the hall. Lily glances around as Savage Sea crew, slaves, and prisoners hold Staunton's soldiers at sword and gun point. Then, she looks from her new wound back up to Jack and takes hold of his arm. "Please, don't let me die in this hell."

"Die? What do you mean? You're going to be fine," Jack replies, fighting to keep his voice steady.

"You're a lot of things Jack Teague, but you are not a liar. Please…"

Jack nods. "Okay." He slips his arms under Lily and lifts her into a cradle hold. As he also becomes aware of the silence in the hall he looks for Knox. "Confiscate their weapons and put them in the cells. Then, get someone up on the parapet to raise a white flag so the rest of the guards know to lay down their arms," he instructs.

Knox nods once as Jack strides to the large double doors leading out to the main entrance of the fort, Lily struggling to help support herself in his arms.

"I've got you," he whispers in her ear and she relaxes into his hold.

They exit without another word.

~

Jack and Lily don't speak as he carries her down the steps and eventually out onto the sand. She simply rests the side of her head where his chest meets his shoulder, listening to the somewhat fast beating of Jack's heart.

The sun's rays have begun peaking over the horizon,

lighting up the sky in beautiful orange and pink hues. He places Lily down near the water's edge, but far enough back to ensure they don't get wet, then sits behind her so she can lean back on him.

"It's beautiful," she wheezes. "Thank you."

"Lily…"

"It's okay," she interrupts, wrapping his free arm around her so his forearm rests lightly across her chest. "You got me out."

"I was meant to save you. Instead, I…"

"You did. You saved me from his torment and a future of being alive but not living." She pauses, squeezing his hand. "Jack, the things he's done to me, the things he'd continue to do…"

Tears are licking the corners of Jack's eyes. "A quick death was too good for him, I should've kept him alive so we could take our time."

"No," Lily interrupts. "I choose to believe he'll suffer for eternity now." She looks up at Jack. There's a silent moment between them. The pain in Lily's eyes tells Jack everything about what it's been like for her here without her having to say a word.

"I'll be forever grateful to you. I know the persona you must portray to survive, but the man underneath is a good one. You showed me kindness when you didn't have to, and you made me believe in something again after three years of torment."

Jack looks away, blinking as tears slowly roll down his face. Lily reaches up, using her fingers to turn his head back to her. Her hands are cold, which sends a slight shiver through his body. When he meets her gaze again

217

she continues.

"I regret nothing, Jack. Do you understand me?"

"I do." His voice becomes gravely as he struggles to hold back the sob rising up his throat. The sadness of finding someone like Lily, only to have her ripped from his life so quickly was grating on him.

Lily coughs forcefully and blood trickles from the side of her mouth. Her breathing is more labored now. Having witnessed this before, there's no doubt in his mind that the pistol's projectile hit one of her lungs. It wouldn't be long now.

"I want you to promise me something," she continues.

"Anything."

Lily looks to the water. "When I'm gone, send me off like a pirate of old. Do not bury me here, let me burn and dissolve into the sea to live forever among the waves."

Jack holds her tighter. "I'd never leave you here."

"Also, and this is the most important... I want you to live without regret. Live knowing you did what no one else could. You freed me. You showed me love, and I ..." Lily's voice trails off as she coughs again.

Jack quickly but gently moves from behind her so he can kneel beside her. "Let me save you," he begs. In his heart he knows there's nothing he can actually do, but he has to say something.

Lily shakes her head slightly. "Jack, we both know there's nothing you can..."

"I can try. Please, don't leave me. You've changed everything for me. You're my heart, remember? I can't live the rest of this life without you."

Lily smiles faintly. "You can, and you will." Her voice is barely a whisper now.

Without hesitating, Jack lifts her head slightly and lowers his, taking Lily's lips in his own. The metallic taste of her blood fills his mouth, but he doesn't stop kissing her. To him, the kiss lasts a blissful eternity, but then he feels her pull away.

"Jack, I," she barely manages to get out before her body goes limp in his arms, the light and life quickly fading from her eyes, accompanying her last breath.

"Lily?" Jack shakes her slightly. There's no change. "No," he moans, lifting her up more and rocking her in his arms. "Not her, please not her!" he exclaims. A mixture of sadness, anger, and heartbreak swells within him as he closes his eyes, holding her tightly in pained silence as the world around him fades away.

He doesn't know how much time passes. Suddenly, Jack opens his eyes, an important conversation between him and Eudora from when he first became Captain, replaying in his mind. "No," he whispers with resolve, "I won't let this happen."

He gently lays Lily back on the sand, wipes his eyes and stands. Jack turns to the sea, rushes to the water's edge, unsheathing his dagger as he goes, then slices his right hand open as he steps into the lapping waves. He rests it on top of the water. "Eudora," he calls softly.

He immediately feels an energy shift and a few moments later, the water in front of him begins to swirl. She appears, taking in the sight of Lily's lifeless body on the sand when she fully materializes.

"Please, save her," he begs.

Eudora sighs. "You know the rules Jack. The balance must be maintained."

"I know, and I'm willing. My soul in exchange for hers. Let her take my place in this world. Let her experience the good after suffering through some of the worst parts of it."

"Why?" Eudora inquires.

"I love her," he responds without hesitation.

"Captain!" Knox calls, eyes wide with concern.

Jack turns back to the beach to see a few members of his crew gathered behind Lily's body. He looks back to Eudora. "Please, accept this trade."

She nods. "It's your decision, made with your own freewill. With the balance maintained I have no reason to object."

"How much time will I have when she wakes?"

"A few minutes at most." She produces a vial from one of her pockets, dips it into the sea to collect some water, then begins whispering an incantation. The water turns a shade of violet. "Pour this into her mouth. I'll be waiting here."

Jack takes the vial then walks back up onto the beach.

"Captain, what's going on?" Knox asks.

Jack approaches his crew. He pauses as he inhales deeply, then opens his mouth to speak. "It's been a great honor serving as your Captain. I could not have asked for a better, more loyal crew. You are the best, and worst crew a Captain could hope for."

Some of the men smirk at his statement, knowing what he means.

Jack continues. "This is something I have to do. Some

of you have wives and families, you know you'd do anything for them." He looks at Lily. "I have to do this for her."

The crew looks from him to Lily, the ones with families nod their heads in agreement.

He focuses on Knox. "Take her to Havara. Keep her safe."

"Of course, Captain," Knox replies.

Jack bids them farewell before going to Lily and kneeling beside her. "It's your turn to live, little flower," he whispers, tilting her head back and pouring the violet liquid into her mouth.

After a few moments, Lily's eyes flutter open and she gasps deeply. She's attempting to get her bearings when her eyes settle on Jack.

"Jack?"

"Hi," he replies, sitting her up.

"What happened?" Lily looks down at her abdomen. There's no more blood or wound. In fact, it doesn't feel like she's been shot at all. She quickly whips her head up at Jack in confusion, then sees Eudora standing just beyond the water's edge in the surf.

"What did you do?" Lily exclaims.

Jack pulls her to her feet. "I don't have much time."

She shakes her head. "No. Jack. You promised!" Lily's heart feels like it's about to burst through her chest into a million pieces as she remembers their conversation about maintaining balance. "How could you?" she pleads.

Jack takes her hands in his. "I've lived enough for one lifetime, and you've barely had the chance. Believe me when I say I would give anything to go through the rest of my life with you. You made me feel things I never thought possible. Despite everything you've been through, you're a true light in this world, Lily Mearas. Live, whatever life you choose for yourself. Embrace adventure, stay in a quiet cottage by the sea, whatever you want. Havara will be your home until you decide."

Lily begins to cry. "Jack, please. If I'm going to do any of that I want to do it with you."

"I wish we could." Jack releases her hands, wrapping her in his arms. He kisses her forehead hard. "You're not broken, do you hear me? You're so strong and you'll find joy. I'll be with you always; every ray of sun that warms your beautiful skin, the breeze in your fiery hair, the gentle waves of the sea that lap at your feet as you walk through them. You'll feel me in everything."

Jack looks to Eudora who gestures for him to follow and he nods. "Promise me," he says, pulling Lily from him so he can look into her eyes.

She shakes her head slowly, to which he responds by pushing his lips tightly against hers with a feverish passion that she returns.

"Jack," Eudora calls.

With much reluctance, Jack pulls away from Lily and cradles her head in his hands. "Live, not for me, but for yourself Lily." He kisses her forehead gently one more time, then turns and walks to the edge of the water.

"Jack!" Lily calls.

He turns in time to catch her as she jumps into his arms and plants another kiss on his lips.

"I promise," she finally replies.

Jack lowers her back onto the sand with a smile. He releases Lily and continues wading out into the sea until he's face-to-face with Eudora. He inhales deeply. "I'm ready."

Eudora holds out her hands, exuding nothing but calmness. Jack takes them gently before she guides him to stand beside her, looking back to the shoreline. Water swirls around their feet then slowly rises, continuing to swirl around them like an orb.

"I love you, little flower," he declares for what he knows will be the final time, eyes locked on Lily.

"I love you, my Captain," she responds in the steadiest voice she can manage.

A moment later the water fully envelopes Jack and Eudora as the golden light from within it shines so brightly it's blinding.

When the water splashes back down onto the sea's surface, they're gone.

Lily's breath catches in her throat and she falls to her knees. Her cries and the gently lapping waves along the shoreline are the only sounds anyone can hear.

After everything, she can't believe this is the end of their story, one that had barely begun. Jack had given up his life for hers and she'd promised to live it fully, but at this moment, she can't imagine keeping that promise.

● ● ●

● ● ●

Did you really think I'd end it there, little flower?

EPILOGUE
FIVE YEARS LATER

George jumps from the skiff into the shallow waters of Havara's shoreline and begins using the rope to pull it farther onto the beach, with Knox still seated in front looking toward the cottage on the hill.

They were a few weeks late and he knew he'd catch a little hell for it, but he smiles at the thought.

"Ready, Captain," George announces.

Knox begins climbing out of the skiff.

George helps steady him on the sand as he works to regain his balance. They share a few silent moments while looking at the Savage Sea anchored further out, sails drawn in, bobbing up and down on the calm waters closer to the bay.

"The crew will be all right, Captain Knox," George states assuringly, knowing his Captain's ready to make this decision.

Knox takes a deep, steadying breath. "I know," he replies softly with a nod.

"Captain Knox!" a sweet, familiar voice exclaims

from behind them.

Knox smiles as the sound reaches his ears. They both turn around and he opens his arms wide. "Jack!" he calls back.

The boy leaps into Knox's arms, the force causing him to stumble back a few steps, but he doesn't lose his balance.

They embrace tightly before the boy maneuvers himself so his face is level with Knox's. "You're late," he states matter of factly with a grimace, but can't maintain the stern look he's attempting to convey and it immediately turns into a giggle.

Knox lowers Jack to the sand and crouches in front of him. "I do apologize lad, our journey ended up taking a little longer than expected." Knox pauses for a moment. At only five, young Jack already looks so much like his father it's startling.

A shadow envelops Jack as his mother approaches.

"Hello Captain Knox… George," she says sweetly to each of them.

Knox stands. "Hello Lily." He steps around Jack to embrace her.

They hold each other tightly.

"It's so good to see you," she continues as they separate and she turns to George to hug him. "We were getting worried, I'm happy to see you both looking so well."

"Hello Lily," George replies, releasing her.

As Lily steps back, Jack moves to his mother's side. Knox looks at both of them, the fullness in his heart overpowering the sadness that had begun to settle over him.

The memory of Lily's pregnancy and the absolute terror she felt all those months - fearing the child was Staunton's - rush back to him.

~

The night his dear wife, Ellie, delivered the baby, Knox paced anxiously in the yard, his mind racing with worry for both Lily and the child. After everything Staunton had done, would she truly want to keep it?

To this day, he couldn't remember every detail of that night, but the moment he heard the transition between Lily's deeper moans and the wails of the newly delivered baby, something in him just knew it was Jack's. When Ellie finally emerged from the cottage, she confirmed his feelings.

"Well?" he asked with much anticipation and anxiety.

The smile on her face was so big. "It's a healthy baby boy," she replied, wiping her freshly washed hands on her apron.

"What about?"

"His hair is as dark as a moonless night, and his skin is a tawny color, just like Jack's," she replied before he could finish asking.

Knox let out a long sigh of relief. Lily was a pale redhead, and Staunton had been just as pale with blonde hair. Knox felt a strange sense of relief that Lily had already been pregnant prior to being captured and taken back to Agrego.

"Small mercies," he whispered.

"Small mercies," Ellie agreed. "Go on, go see them."

Knox entered Lily's bedroom slowly as his eyes fell on the new mother seated on her bed, cradling a baby in her arms.

Lily looked up and smiled when she caught sight of him, eyes brimming with tears. "Come. Come meet the newest crew member of the Savage Sea," she teased.

Knox chuckled as he walked to the side of the bed, taking a seat on the small stool his wife had left there.

The boy was wrapped in a thin blanket, but Lily angled her arms so Knox could see him. One look at that precious face and any lingering doubts that the child might not be Jack's were gone. "He looks so much like Jack," he remarked without thinking.

Lily continued to hold back her tears. "He does." The relief in her voice was unmistakable. "His name's Jack, in honor of his father."

Knox was teary-eyed now. "A perfect name."

"I guess I know now what the witch on Agrego meant when she told me to drink the healing elixir for 'what's inside.' I don't know how she knew I was with child, but despite everything she helped do to me, I'm grateful she knew."

~

"Captain Knox, are you okay?" Lily asks, breaking through the haze of the memory he was lost in, and bringing him back to the present.

Knox blinks a few times and smiles back at her. "Yes, perfectly."

"Come on," Jack declares, taking Knox's hand, starting to guide him up the beach toward the dunes. "I want to hear everything," he continues excitedly.

The four of them walk slowly up the little hill to the house, Knox and Jack speaking excitedly while Lily and George walk behind, speaking in slightly hushed tones.

"Tell me, George. How is he, really? He seems different."

"Honestly, the Captain hasn't been quite the same since Ellie passed, but I know seeing you and little Jack is doing his soul good."

"Mama!" Jack calls.

"What is it, sweetie?"

"Captain Knox says he has a surprise for us from his adventure!" Jack is giddy with excitement.

"That's so thoughtful! Did you thank him?"

"I will. But he says I won't see it until tomorrow."

Lily smiles. "Well, I for one can't wait to find out what it is."

"Me too!" Jack beams, turning back around and taking Knox's hand as they approach the house.

"You need to stop bringing him things, you all spoil him," she whispers to George.

He grins. "You try telling Knox that."

They both chuckle.

After they all finish their stew, and Knox and George

have regaled Jack with a few stories from their latest adventure, Knox looks out the window. It's after sunset, only a few short hours until the full moon reaches its peak in the sky.

"Be honest with me," Lily says softly, taking a seat next to him. "Are you all right? You seem distant."

Knox smiles, giving her hand a gentle squeeze. "Never better my dear, never better."

They all continue chatting as the minutes tick by. It's clear Jack is fighting sleep, but eventually it overwhelms him and George lays him in his bed.

"So, what's this surprise you have for my son?" Lily inquires now that the boy's asleep.

Knox and George exchange glances then nod at each other.

"Okay, now you're scaring me, what's going on?" Lily asks, unease settling within her.

Knox looks over at her as he removes the pouch from around his neck. "Sweet Lily, nothing is wrong. In fact, it's all about to be made right again," he sighs.

Her brow furrows. "What are you talking about?"

Knox rises, holding a hand out to her. "Come, walk with me. George will stay here with Jack."

Lily takes his hand and they walk out the front door. *"Leave it to pirates to be so cryptic,"* she thinks.

George settles into his chair, tipping back so he's leaning against the wall. Within minutes he's snoring gently.

Their walk down the hill to the beach is silent, but when they reach the sand Lily finally breaks it. "Captain Knox, please tell me what's going on."

Knox takes a deep breath as he opens the pouch and carefully removes a corked vial. The soft golden glow from within is now visible to Lily, who stops short.

"What is that?"

"It took us a little longer than anticipated, but we finally found all the ingredients," he replies.

"Ingredients for what?"

Knox's expression softens.

A sense of fear rises within her. "What have you done? Or rather, what are you planning to do?"

Knox continues walking to the shoreline a short distance away as he uncorks the vial. "I'm righting a wrong," he replies.

"What are you talking about?" Lily's beside him now, the cool ocean water lapping at their feet.

Knox looks from the vial to Lily. "I can bring him back," he states quietly.

Lily gasps. "What?" she asks, eyes wide.

"This is what we've been looking for these last two years. I now have all the ingredients needed to summon Eudora and bring Jack back."

"But... how? I mean, Jack never officially passed you the captaincy so I thought the bond with her was broken. Also, she was very clear, a life for a life, to maintain the balance. I died on that beach, Jack exchanging his life for mine was..." Realization hits her. "Oh no, Captain Knox, please, you can't."

Knox continues looking out at the ocean. "I'm ready. I miss my dear Ellie and want nothing more than to be reunited with her. If I can do so while also returning Jack to you and your son, well, there would be nothing better I could ever do for any of you. That boy deserves his father, and you more than deserve to be with the man you love. You all belong together, a family."

Lily's heart pounds, feeling like it'll burst through her ribs at any moment. "Are you sure this will work?"

He chuckles lightly and nods.

"And you're sure it's not breaking any rules?"

"I'm healthy Lily, it's not my natural time yet, so it's a fair exchange." He turns to her. "Now, you tell young Jack how much I love him, that I've gone on the ultimate adventure far away, and I'll always be with him."

Lily's tears have broken through their barrier and roll softly down her face. "I will," she promises.

Knox takes both her hands in his and kisses the tops of them. "It's been an absolute honor to know you."

With that, he lets go and turns to face the sea. The moon is now at its pinnacle in the sky and is so bright it casts a perfect circle of light down on the water. Knox wades into the center of the reflection and pours the contents of the vial into the sea. The water in front of him starts to bubble and rise in a column as Eudora materializes.

"Captain Knox."

"Hello Eudora," he replies.

"You've finished your quest."

"I have, and I'm ready. I make this decision freely."

Eudora glances at the shoreline, having spotted Lily. "I understand," she responds with a nod. She takes his empty vial, dips it into the sea and repeats the same incantation from five years ago. When the water turns violet she hands it to Knox.

He downs it.

Eudora offers him her hands. "Take them."

Knox does as instructed. As soon as his hands are in hers the water around them begins to swirl and rise in a sphere until it envelops both of them, just like it did to Jack five years ago. He takes a steadying breath and closes his eyes, happily envisioning Ellie.

Lily watches from the shore, barely breathing. Knox and Eudora are fully enveloped now and the water's glowing a brilliant gold.

Suddenly, the sphere falls back to the surface and the perfect glow of the moon returns. Lily gasps at the figure now standing in the middle of the moon's reflection and she recognizes him immediately. She says "Jack" so softly she questions whether or not she truly said it.

Jack looks up, a little confused. The last time he saw her was on a beach very different from this one and it was dawn, not the middle of the night. He remembers the way she looked at him as he faded away, then nothing. "Lily?"

After a moment they run toward each other, stopping when they're face to face, looking at one another in disbelief.

Jack reaches out cupping her face in his hands. "Is this real?" he asks breathlessly. "How long has it been?"

Lily nods, letting the weight of her head settle into his palms while she wraps her own hands around his and more tears well in her eyes. "Five years."

Jack starts to breathe deeply as if the feel of her face

is confirmation that he's not somehow dreaming. He pulls her into him, their lips meeting. The passion they felt for one another five years ago blossoms as if no time has passed at all and he soaks in every moment of her mouth on his.

"How?" he asks, forcing himself to break the kiss.

"I'll tell you everything, I promise," she weeps, running her fingers through his hair, pulling his face back down to hers.

"Mama?" a soft voice calls from behind her.

Lily turns quickly and her eyes immediately fall on her son, who's standing along the dunes, his eyes wide, unsure of what he just witnessed. She glances up at Jack, whose gaze flickers between the young boy and her. She takes a steadying breath before stepping out of his embrace and going to her son.

When she reaches young Jack she kneels down in front of him, taking his little hands in hers.

"Who is that?" he asks quietly, still cautious of the stranger who stands before him.

Lily smiles softly. "It's okay. There's someone I want you to meet."

She guides him back to Jack, who has moved out of the water and now stands completely on the sand, his mouth slightly open in what appears to be confusion.

Lily looks at the man she's loved for the past five years, then down at her son as she says, "Do you remember the story I told you about your father? And that in order to save mommy he had to go away?"

The boy nods enthusiastically. "Yes, and that even though we couldn't see him, he was always with us and we'd see him again one day."

"That's right. Well, this is the surprise Captain Knox had for you. Jack, this is your father."

Jack can see the boy's face clearly now in the light of the full moon, and the resemblance is unmistakable, he looks almost identical to how he looked as a child.

Lily sniffles and clears her throat while looking back at her love. "My Captain, meet your son, Jack."

A barrage of thoughts and feelings hit Jack all at once, as does the immediate realization that this is not the time or place to ask Lily in front of their son, so he simply kneels in front of him instead. "Hello Jack," he practically whispers, tears partially obscuring his vision.

The young boy looks at him a few moments, still holding onto his mother's hand. A wide smile spreads across his tiny face and wordlessly, the boy jumps into Jack's arms, hugging him tightly around the neck.

Jack wraps his arms around his son and rises.

Lily covers her mouth while her tears fall freely.

Jack looks over to her and holds out his free hand. "Come here, *my* flower," he beckons softly.

She takes it without hesitation and he pulls her into the hug. There's so much to say, however, at this moment, none of it matters.

For now, the two of them stand on the sand, their son nestled between them, content with the knowledge that after everything, the life they'd wanted together five years ago is just beginning.

ABOUT THE AUTHOR

Alyssa Romeo is a self-published author with a lifelong love of storytelling. As a child, she often filled her diary with imaginative tales rather than daily events - a habit that evolved into a passion for writing fiction. Her debut two-part novel series, *The Wish* (2013) and *Always* (2014), marked her first foray into the world of publishing.

Alyssa writes whenever she can find the time and travels as often as possible, often gathering inspiration for her stories when she does. She also enjoys spending time with her dog (the perfect companion for those long writing sessions), and making memories with her family and friends.

Follow Alyssa on Instagram & TikTok
@alyssaromeoauthor

www.ingramcontent.com/pod-product-compliance
Lightning Source LLC
Chambersburg PA
CBHW032028120726
47901CB00002BA/498